THE RIDGE

By

Thomas Blenk

ISBN: 0-7596-9373-0 (Electronic)
ISBN: 0-7596-9374-9 (Softcover)

This book is printed on acid free paper.

1stBooks – rev. 09/26/02

Mike Sullivan glanced at the revolving sign over carousel B.
—Flight 1175—

"Let the crowd gather, then move in," he said.

Sully glanced at the rest of his party. They could have been any group of friends returning from a vacation, but they had not been on flight 1175. The four men and two women were here for a pick-up.

A buzzer sounded and the bags started out of the chute.

Four golf bags and two duffel bags, Mike thought. Get the bags, get the van, and hit the road.

Sully stood 6'1" and weighed 225 pounds. Normally he dressed in jeans, sweatshirt and a baseball cap, but not today. Today he was playing the part of a golfer, wearing a polo shirt, shorts, and a straw hat to hide his shoulder length hair.

He had been in and out of jail since the age of twelve, but if they could pull this off, he would be set for life. The payoff would be almost two million dollars. Just get the stuff to New Mexico and make the exchange.

The cocaine was loaded in Columbia. Baggage handlers in most airports can be bribed: in Columbia it is a way of life.

In the world of baggage claim, there are three distinctive groups of people. The first group, consisting of one or more people, go directly to the opening where the bags originate and stay there until their bags pop out.

The second scenario can also involve more than one person. This group arrives at any spot on the carousel to wait patiently until each bag comes around.

The third group splits the duties. One or more people stays with the group's belongings while others travel back and forth until all bags can be retrieved.

Sully's group fell into the third category. He stood off to one side with Donna and his sister, Caitlin. The others waited at the revolving belt.

"Come on. Let's go," Sully muttered to himself. Why did it seem when you stood at one of these things your bags always came out last? And why was Caitlin so nervous? he thought.

Caitlin Sullivan, a slightly overweight, plain looking brunette, seemed older than her years. She stood wringing her hands and

1

shifting her weight from one foot to the other. Her eyes darted from Sully, to Donna, to the baggage belt and back again. She had worked with him a dozen times before, but today she was driving him nuts. He stepped close and whispered.

"What the hell is wrong with you? Will you take it easy?"

Caitlin forced a smile. "Ok! Ok! I'm just nervous, Sully."

They were not your ordinary brother and sister act.

Mike and Caitlin grew up on the Lower East Side of New York City. It was a family filled with poverty, alcoholism, and abuse. Their parents fought and drank, and the old man beat them all. It was no great loss when he drove his truck head-on into a telephone pole on New Years Eve, 1973. The cops said he was traveling at least eighty miles an hour, and his blood alcohol level was 2.1.

The old lady's answer to her husband's death was to turn her children over to the state. They moved from foster home to foster home, and Caitlin soon turned to drugs. By the age of thirteen, she was hooked.

Mike turned out much tougher, but no better off. A series of petty crimes led to a juvenile felony conviction in 1976. He might have fared better if he had not beaten the store manager half to death with a handgun.

You can learn a lot in juvenile detention, and Sully paid attention.

While in Juvee he met Robert "Bo" Boston. They were both inner city kids and hit it off right away. In prison each watched the other's back while they made plans for the future. Bo was the one person in the world that Sully trusted.

The three years passed, and he wasted little time resuming his life's work. Sully spent the next few years selling drugs, pimping whores, and fronting one robbery after another. Convicted of car theft in 1984, he served five years in federal prison. Less than eight months later, he was back, and as a three time loser, he got fifteen to twenty in the state pen.

He served seven years before being released on parole because of good behavior. Sully was determined to go straight, but that only lasted until he got sick of menial jobs, no money and no fun. That's when the call came from Richie.

Sully met Richie Gomez in 1985. Richie was in for armed robbery. He and his brother, Ron, robbed a deli on Seventy-eighth

Street. They got away with two hundred thirty bucks and some change. The cops were after them within hours. Ron Gomez slipped out of the city and headed for his uncle's place in New Mexico. Richie was not so lucky. The cops showed up while he was packing.

Six years later after being released from prison, he left New York to join his brother.

When he called, Richie told a story of a multi-million dollar deal. They needed someone to pick up the goods and deliver them to New Mexico.

"This is a good deal, Sully. You always talked about the big score. Well, this is it. What do you say?" Richie said.

Sully said yes and then started looking for a crew.

Bo was the best wheelman Sully knew. He could drive or fly anything that had a motor, and he loved the action. Bo had to be in.

Larry Webster, a tall, slightly built man, met Sully on Sully's last trip to prison. Webster's gambling habit kept him on the wrong side of the law. He took any bet offered, even the flip of a coin. He bet on college and pro sports, frequenting Vegas, Tahoe, and Atlantic City. Craps, poker, blackjack—it didn't matter to Webster as long as there was a bet involved. Like most gamblers, he lost more than he won. He needed money to pay his debts and money to feed his addiction, leading to various run-ins with the law.

To Sully, it only mattered that Webster knew firearms. An expert marksman who could assemble and dismantle almost any weapon would be a good man to have on the job.

Jimmy Kann was big, scary, dangerous, and not too bright, but he was loyal. He would do what he was told while on the job. The problem with Jimmy was his penchant for women. Twice charged with rape and three times with assault, his lawyers had somehow kept him out of prison. Sully knew Kann had to be watched.

Donna, Bo's girlfriend, would be the other female in the group. They needed a second woman, and Bo wanted Donna. Donna was excited. She had been in plenty of tight spots in her call girl days, but this would be different. This, she decided, would be fun.

Sully glanced one more time around the baggage claim area of Kennedy Airport. There were three carousels: A, B, and C. Each one was surrounded by an assortment of people—families with kids,

3

couples returning from vacation, and business travelers moving from one transaction to another.

He saw nothing out of the ordinary. Sully was not expecting any trouble, but over the years, he had become a very careful man.

Bo caught his attention. The bags were up.

*   *   *   *   *

Detective Collins looked like every other businessman in the baggage claim area. He wore a navy blue suit with a laptop computer slung over his shoulder. Anyone watching him would see a man late and frustrated. His two cell phone calls made it obvious that he was late for an important meeting downtown.

In reality, Collins was keeping an eye on four men and two women at carousel B.

When they had their bags and headed for the elevators, he punched the buttons on his phone for the third time.

"Frank, they've got their stuff and are headed your way. I'll stay with them to the elevators, and then call you again," he said.

Collins pocketed his phone and started after the six suspects.

Chapter 2

Cal Mitchell wondered how he had gotten so old. He watched from the far side of the hangar as Jan, Chris, and Amy loaded the plane from the cargo hold door.

Jan can't really be fifty, he thought. She doesn't look a day over thirty. If she's fifty then I'm forty-nine, and that can't be! Of course, it is true both kids are over twenty-five, and we've been married for thirty years.

He was on his way to take a shower when he paused to watch Jan. A lot of men stopped to watch Jan Mitchell.

She wore jeans and a short-sleeved chamois shirt cut to her waist, accentuating her toned, athletic body. Her shoulder-length reddish brown hair was done up in a ponytail, making her look even younger.

Cal sighed and reached for his gym bag. He and Jan had certainly come a long way together.

*   *   *   *   *

He first saw her thirty-two years earlier at a high school football game in Connecticut. She caught his eye as he jogged off the field at the end of the game. Jan was beautiful in the red, white, and blue colors of the opposing team, and Cal knew he was in love. They actually met two days later, when he applied for a job as a busboy at a local restaurant where Jan was a waitress. That June they went to her senior prom, and as they say, "The rest is history."

They were married right out of high school, in the summer of 1969, and decided that Jan would finish school first. Two things changed their plans and the rest of their lives. Cal was drafted in January of 1970, and two months later, Jan announced that she was pregnant. He shipped out in August, and the baby was born in December. Jan finished school and started to raise their daughter while he went to fight a war he knew nothing about in a place he had never heard of.

In February of 1973 he returned home—Captain Mitchell, commander of the most decorated Special Forces unit of the war. He led seventeen missions behind enemy lines, and he killed to stay alive and protect his men. He was awarded five combat citations, including the Medal of Honor. Like most men who have tasted the horrors of combat, Cal had no desire to relive it. He never talked about Vietnam, even to Jan. After a while, the nightmares went away.

Six months after his return, Cal got a call from Richard Ireland. Ireland, an Assistant Director with The CIA, was putting together an elite group of six men who would answer directly to him. They would be handsomely paid to act in the best interests of the United States, as seen through the eyes of Richard Ireland. Only a handful of people would know they existed and, depending on the operation, even Ireland could disavow knowledge of their actions.

The money seemed too good to turn down and, for the next seven years, he worked for the government.

Jan never liked the decision. She knew it was the CIA, and it didn't take long for the job to take a toll on them. The constant travel and worry drove her further and further away. If he wanted to hold his marriage together, he would have to make a change.

While undercover in 1975, he heard about a young man named Bill Gates. He had developed something called BASIC, the programming language for his first microcomputer. Cal kept track of Gates and started investing slowly in something called Microsoft. By 1980, he and his partner, Skip Amanski, were ready to go out on their own. They formed SKIPCAL CORPORATION and, one year later, they were off and running.

Today they were a billion dollar Wall Street success story. SKIPCAL became one of the best known and well respected companies the world over.

None of that mattered to Cal as they prepared the plane for this trip. Traci is getting married in two days, and we'd better be there for tomorrow's rehearsal, he thought. Thank God I asked Billy to do the flying. I'm too nervous. Just the thought of having to walk down the aisle with his oldest daughter made his knees weak.

He took one last look at Jan as she passed a duffel bag to Amy.

"Jan, I'm hitting the shower before we go," he said.

"Okay. Billy called in the flight plan already. We don't take off until 3:30, so you've got plenty of time. Don't take forever, though. We still have to do a final flight check," Jan replied.

Cal turned at the bathroom door and laughed.

"The only way that happens is if you join me!"

"You guys want to be left alone?" Chris said, standing and grinning in the cargo hold doorway.

Jan blushed a deep crimson. "Sorry, honey. We have company."

"Story of my life," Cal said, shaking his head and heading for the hangar men's room.

Chapter 3

Frank Martini felt tired. He always seemed tired these days and, with his receding hairline and expanding waistline, he looked the part. He was fifty-two with thirty years in as a New York City cop. He started his career walking a beat in Harlem but quickly worked his way up the ladder. He had always wanted to be a cop, and he gained an early reputation as a tough, but fair, officer. After only five years on the job, he had his detective shield.

Martini's job took him from vice, to drug enforcement, to homicide. To him, the drug pushers were the worst; they preyed on the weak and never showed any remorse. He saw too many people strung out or dead because of the stuff they brought into his city.

Right now, his interest centered on just such a group and the stakeout he set up to catch them.

Martini hated stakeouts, especially those based on the word of an informant. Today the feeling was a little different. He believed this snitch. He believed something big was about to happen.

The original call came in two days earlier, and she asked for him specifically. The woman told him that she knew he had arrested her brother nine years earlier, and she needed his help. Her name was Caitlin, and her brother was Mike Sullivan. He, of course, remembered both of them. Twice, he was the arresting officer involving Mike Sullivan. She told him that her brother was involved in a big drug deal at Kennedy Airport. She refused to help at first, but Mike would not listen.

Martini thought about the siblings for a moment. Mike was trouble, and one more conviction would put him away for good. Caitlin, on the other hand, was harmless—a loser, but harmless. She asked for his protection, and he saw no problem letting her go if her information panned out.

He took one last look around the Avis Rent-a-Car desk. Every angle he could think of was covered. Collins had just called, and the show was about to begin. The people behind the car rental desks were working for him, and he had their full attention as he spoke.

"Heads up! Quick review. We're looking for six people—four men and two women. They're probably armed and dangerous. They'll be carrying four golf bags and other assorted luggage." Martini paused for a moment.

"Treat them all the same. We don't want to give the sister away as a snitch. Sullivan knows me, so I will stay out of sight until they are off the elevators. Any questions?"

"Okay. Let's take our places."

Chapter 4

Carrie loved the early hours on the ranch. The change from dead quiet to full blown activity was almost palpable. She sat on the porch railing sipping from a steaming mug of black coffee. The morning air was crisp as she watched the sun come up on the horizon where the sky seemed to turn different shades of amber.

Today the stock would be boarded and shipped to the coast for the Grand National Rodeo. She still could not bring herself to go back to the show in San Francisco. "Was it seven years ago that I decided to stay home?" she asked herself.

Rory went with the rest of the crew, and she never saw him alive again. The doctors said it was a massive brain aneurysm, and he died instantly. They said she never would have had a chance to say goodbye. "I should have been there anyway," she told herself for the millionth time. The pain got dull after a while, but it never went away.

She met Rory Douglas on a dude ranch a hundred miles from the *Circle R.* It made you wonder about fate. She was a twenty-two year old from a well to do family in upstate New York, visiting Arizona on a lark. After graduation, Carrie and her college friends decided to take a vacation together before moving on with their lives. Why they settled on a ranch in the Arizona desert instead of, say, the South of France, is hard to fathom.

Their first morning on the ranch, an eighteen wheeler from the *Circle R* arrived.,Rory Douglas was a vision of the western cowboy when he stepped down from the cab. He was tall and lean with a rock hard body burnt dark by the sun. His face was chiseled and angular. He tipped his sweat-stained Stetson to the girls while never letting his blue eyes leave Carrie's face.

Caroline Martin and Rory Douglas came from entirely different worlds.

She grew up in Cortland, New York, thirty miles south of Syracuse. The Martins lived in a nice, upper middle-class neighborhood, where Caroline was a popular fun-loving child. She attended Saint Michael's Elementary School and then on to Cortland Middle and High school. She excelled in school, both socially and academically: on the honor roll for four years, class secretary in her junior and senior years, and an All-State basketball and lacrosse player as a senior.

Caroline was also popular with the boys, dating regularly through her junior year. That summer, she started going steady with Tommy Garrett. Also that summer, she lost her virginity, smothered in excitement and curiosity, convinced that they were in love forever. The dream faded long before graduation.

Her grades were good enough to get her into Rutgers, where she studied, worked, partied, and had a few minor romances. She had a blast. The last two years were the best. Living in an off campus house with her six roommates were times she would never forget. Together, they chose the western adventure.

Rory came from a family of cowboys. It was a tough, hard-working life, and though he loved it, he decided early on that someday he would own a ranch of his own. To do that he needed money and, at the age of twelve, he entered his first junior calf-roping contest. Seven years later he was a world champion. By the time he was twenty-five, he had won five titles and retired as owner of the *Circle R*.

The day they met, Rory was supposed to be at the Lazy-K Dude Ranch long enough to drop off livestock. All the vacationers came out to see them unload the truck. That's when he saw her, and that's when he decided to stay the night.

He returned three times in the next two weeks and invited the girls to visit the *Circle R*. They spent their last two days in Arizona watching a working ranch in action. When it came time to leave, Rory asked Carrie to stay.

Carrie knew it was crazy. Her friends told her she was nuts, but whenever he was near, she felt weak, with a fainting feeling deep inside. She decided to stay.

Rory showed her everything about his way of life, and they spent each evening on Culverton Ridge watching the sunset. They made love for the first time on a bedroll on the ridge, and it was the most gentle, romantic moment of her life.

That was seventeen years ago, and she could still see his face at times like this in the pre-dawn haze, or whenever she ventured up to the ridge to watch the sunset.

"Morning, Mrs. Douglas." Brett, the ranch foreman said. "Just wondering if we're sending all four bulls or keeping Jessup behind."

Caroline was so deep in thought that she did not see Brett come around the corner.

"Sorry. What? Oh, yeah. Has Jim looked at him this morning?"

"He's down there now, ma'am." Brett replied.

"Well, let's go see what Doc has to say," Carrie said, as she jumped down from the porch.

As the sun crept up on the horizon, Carrie and her foreman headed for the main barn and the vet's best guess on the health of the *Circle R*'s prize rodeo bull.

Chapter 5

Sully felt good as he and his entourage headed for the elevators. He had been involved in enough deals to know not to trust anyone, and the fact that he was dealing with Richie Gomez and some drug lord halfway across the country did not help him sleep nights. So far, so good, though. The bags had arrived on schedule. Obviously they hadn't been able to check the contents right there in the airport, but he was pretty confident of what he had. Five minutes later they stood fifty feet from the elevators, and Sully's good feelings had disappeared.

"Shit, I can't believe this," Kann muttered.

In front of them, a group of wheelchair bound people were being helped into the elevators. The elevators could handle two chairs at a time.

There must be thirty of them, Sully thought. This will take forever. He quickly made a decision to take an alternate route.

"This will take all day. Let's use the stairs we just passed. Down two flights, then there's an escalator straight down to the rental desks."

*   *   *   *   *

Martini stuck his head out from the back room. They should be coming through the elevator doors any second, he thought.

Sully reached the top of the escalator before anyone else. He stopped dead in his tracks. Something was wrong.

Eleven o'clock on a Thursday morning in Kennedy Airport, and there were no lines at the car rental desks. One person in each line at Avis, Hertz, and Budget. And no real movement. No one dragging bags or kids around.

"Something's not right. It's too quiet," he said.

"Come on, Sully," Caitlin said. "You're getting paranoid."

Sully hesitated. He had a feeling, and he didn't like it. Just then he saw movement below to his right. A tall, black man in a suitcoat hanging back out of sight. He had seen him before. Where? Then it hit him. At the baggage claim at the next carousel over, talking on a cell phone.

"I knew it! They're cops, and they're waiting for us. We gotta find another way out. Come on," Sully whispered in a tight voice as he turned toward the stairs.

Sully's mind was racing. How did they know? They were waiting for us. Somehow they found out ahead of time. Focus! If they had the cars covered, they would have buses and taxis covered, too. What else? Fly? No way, every gate would be watched. Suddenly, he stopped and stared out the window at the runway.

"That's the answer," he said. "Stay here. I'll be right back." He walked to the next gate to find an airline attendant. In a few minutes, he was back.

"Let's go. I think I found a way out."

Chapter 6

Jan took one step up and handed the presents to Amy. It was the last of the items to go on the plane and, after handing them to Chris, Amy climbed into the cargo hold to help store the gear.

As she leaned the stepladder against the wall, Jan stopped to listen to the sound of water running in the bathroom. Smiling, she realized that twenty years ago she would have been in the shower with her husband. Well, that was twenty years ago, she thought. Staring at the bathroom door, she visualized him in there, naked. His body still made her weak in the knees. He was the only man who ever made her feel that way. He was the only man she ever loved.

There was that one time when Cal was still an agent and always away. She had opened her art gallery, SKETCHES, and, between working 10 hours a day, bringing up two kids, and Cal being gone for weeks at a time, she had become lonely and vulnerable.

She met him on one of her buying trips for the gallery. He was an artist and very interested in her work and, eventually, in her. She never loved him, although at the time she convinced herself she did. She never completely forgave herself either for almost losing Cal. He confronted her one Friday a year after the affair ended. She never knew how he found out and, for almost a week, she didn't hear from him. She didn't know if he was coming back at all.

The day he returned, she thought he had come to get his stuff, but he didn't leave. He told her he thought life without her would be worse than the pain she had caused. He loved her, and he was staying. Things were strained for awhile, but gradually they became stronger together than ever.

Jan's galleries became her passion. SKETCHES now had four locations: New York, San Francisco, Chicago and, only this year, Paris. Each shop consisted of different display rooms. Upon entering the foyer, patrons found an array of famous artwork. Beyond the foyer were four rooms dedicated to different forms of art from both established and beginning artists. Sculptures, watercolors, oils, and pen and ink drawings from around the world filled the rooms. These, along with some of her own works, were always on site, but Jan was most proud of her program to promote new talent. Every two years, SKETCHES offered grants to young artists in each of the four fields. The applications came in by the thousands, and four were chosen at each location.

The back of each shop contained a small boarding house with a community kitchen and bath. They each had their own living quarters but shared a large workroom where the students were free to pursue their craft without the worry of finances or interruption. One of the biggest events in the art world happened at the end of each two year period when the works of these newcomers went on display at the SKETCHES opening. Every big name art dealer and collector in the world came to these shows. In her wildest dreams, she could not have imagined the success or enjoyment that she found in SKETCHES.

The last few years were wonderful, almost as it was in the beginning—before the kids were born. Traci and Chris graduated from college and moved on with their lives. Chris and Amy married last summer, and now it was Traci's turn. Turning fifty had not been easy, yet she felt younger than ever. They both spent less time at work and more time together. Life was good.

Jan shook her head and headed for the front of the plane. If I think about him anymore, I'll be naked in that shower, too, and we will be late, she thought.

Chapter 7

Martini gave Detective Collins a piercing look as he stepped out from behind the car rental desk. The look said, "What the hell is going on." Collins answered with palms up and a shrug of his shoulders. He had no clue. One half hour ago he called in to say that the packages arrived, and the group in question was on the move. As instructed, he followed at a good distance until they stepped into the elevator corridor. He then doubled back to the car rental desks to report. He gave his boss the thumbs up as he stationed himself below the escalator where he could watch the elevators and not be seen. They should have been here twenty minutes ago, he thought as he watched the anger grow in his boss's eyes. From the time Collins took his position, the doors to the elevators opened seven times. Each time, a wheelchair was pushed out and taken out a side door to a waiting bus.

Martini hadn't stationed anyone in the upstairs elevator area for fear that he might tip his hand. Now he was regretting the decision. He ripped the walkie-talkie from his sports coat pocket and started spitting out orders.

"Check the elevators first. Stay put at all other modes of transportation. We are going to spread out from here and search this entire airport. Take nothing for granted. Six people with that much luggage have to find transportation somewhere."

Martini's people gathered around him and waited for instructions.

"Spread out through each concourse in two man teams. They have to be here somewhere. We have every way out covered. If you spot them, do not approach without backup. Call it in. We will find a safe spot to take them. We don't want a shoot out or a hostage situation. Understood? Okay, Collins, you're with me. Let's go."

Martini's mind was racing as they headed for the escalators. Maybe Caitlin Sullivan lied to him. Maybe the car reservation in Donna Murry's name was a decoy.

No! It doesn't make sense. Why call me at all if she is going to give me false information? Maybe Sullivan found out about his sister ratting him out and made other plans. Again, no logic. If Sullivan knew about her, she would never have made it to the airport, and Collins said she was there for the pick-up.

Something happened between baggage claim and the rental desk to change their plans. Martini was convinced of it. He didn't know why, but he knew the playing field had changed.

Martini looked back at the elevator doors from the moving escalator with the growing feeling that his stakeout was going sour in a hurry.

Chapter 8

Before he even undressed, Cal forced himself to stop thinking about Jan naked in a shower with him. She could still arouse him with just a look or a touch. In fact, she always said it was one of the things she loved most about him, but if she wasn't coming in—and she wasn't—then what was the point of daydreaming about it.

Instead Cal willed himself to think about the flight, the wedding, and the long weekend ahead. Billy was flying, so he didn't have to worry there. The wedding was the girls' department; he just needed to show up and do as he was told. As for the rest of the weekend, I'm just going to play as much golf as possible, he thought.

Well, the wedding might be a little different. He never had to walk down the aisle and give his little girl away and, no matter what, Traci would always be his little girl. He still had to remind himself that she owned her own business and that she was about to be married. To him she would always be the little girl who sat in daddy's lap to watch the Wizard of Oz. Watching the Wizard of Oz was a family tradition, but she was too scared of the witch to sit alone. As the hot water scorched his back, he smiled and remembered.

After showering, Cal threw on boxers and a T-shirt, grabbed a towel, and stepped out of the bathroom drying his hair. As he did, he was staring down the barrel of a 357 Magnum pointed between his eyes.

"You make a sound, you die," Sully whispered.

Immediately Cal assessed the situation, looking first at the cargo door of the plane. He hoped that his family might see what was happening and call for help. That would not be the case—the door was closed. He turned his attention to the intruders.

Four men and two women, and the men all carried weapons. The leader was in front of him with the Magnum. He was Cal's height, bulkier, but about the same weight. Everyone else was looking to him for their next move. A tall, lanky man stood by the door of the plane holding a Russian-made Bizon-2 machine pistol, and Cal could tell he was good with it just by the way he held it.

19

A big, muscle-bound guy stood at the door to the hangar holding a Glock 9mm. He had a mean, dangerous look.

A shorter, balding guy with a Beretta stood over a pile of travel bags. Whatever these guys wanted, it had to do with those bags, Cal thought.

Both women were over by the west wall waiting to be told what to do. The blonde was smiling with an excited look on her face. The other, the brunette, just looked scared.

As his gaze went back to the man in front of him, Cal slowed his breathing and forced his mind to focus. It amazed him that his old training still clicked in automatically.

"What do you want?" Cal asked.

Sully's eyes narrowed. "I'll ask the questions. How many people on the plane?"

Cal hesitated.

"Don't screw with me, pal. How many?"

"Four, including the pilot," Cal finally answered.

"Who are they?"

"My wife, son, daughter-in-law and, like I said, the pilot."

"Where's the plane heading and how soon?" Sully asked.

"Arizona. We're scheduled to leave for Tucson at 3:30."

Sully glanced at his watch. Four hours to wait. His first thought was to leave as soon as possible, but then he caught himself. Be patient and don't bring attention to yourself, two things he had learned to live by when trying to avoid the cops.

"Good. We're hopping a ride. No one gets hurt if we don't get any trouble. We leave you guys and go our merry way when we land. Understood?"

"Understood." Cal understood all too well that his family and Billy's health depended entirely on what these guys were into and how he handled the situation.

"Listen, this is my plane. I can get you money and fly you wherever you want to go. Just let the others leave," Cal offered. "That's all I ask."

Sullivan pushed the gun up against Cal's temple.

"I don't need any suggestions from you. You think I'm stupid? Ten minutes after we leave, the cops are on our ass. So just shut up, and let's go meet the loved ones."

SKIPCAL purchased its first plane, a Lear Jet, for business reasons in 1983. Four years later they moved up to a Boeing 727. They decided not only could they move business passengers from city to city, but also cargo from off-shoot companies they formed. At that time, SKIPCAL also purchased a lease on the hangar at Kennedy Airport that they recently renewed. Finally, in 1990, they settled on a Boeing 737 and customized it to handle all facets of the company.

It was a rare occurrence for the Mitchell's or the Amanski's to use the company plane for personal use, but this was a special occasion.

As he approached the big plane with SKIPCAL emblazoned on the side, Cal felt helpless. He was glad Skip's family was not with them on this trip. He knew his own family was in trouble and his mind was racing, trying to think of a way to protect them and get them out.

Sullivan wanted a small plane like the one he had seen on the runway earlier. The information he got from an airline attendant told him that any private plane arriving would have to taxi to the far west end of the airport to the private hangars.

He decided they would take the first hangar with a plane inside. They would then wait it out until someone came to fly it.

"Okay pal, you first. Remember, I'm right behind you. If I have to start shooting, you will be first, but you won't be the last. Get it?" he said to Cal.

Cal nodded and headed up the temporary steps followed closely by his captors. Sully quickly pushed Cal to the side and stepped through the doorway into the passageway. The cockpit was to his left and the seating section to the right. He faced a small kitchen area and a normal airline bathroom on one side, along with a small storage space opposite.

"Bo, check the cockpit. If the pilot is in there, make sure he understands what's going on," Sullivan said. Then he motioned to Cal and the curtain to his right.

"You lead the way."

They stepped into what seemed like a well-furnished living room, complete with a large wrap-around couch and two reclining chairs. Padded folding chairs hung by hooks attached to the right wall below the windows. The back of the room had a table attached to the wall in the same manner. A wet bar stood at the other end of the room next to a door that led to a sleep area and, farther back, to the cargo hold. On the wall, left of where they entered, was a large screen TV that went the length of the wall. The entire room was covered with plush carpeting. Larry Webster whistled.

"Man, so this is how the rich people live."

"Wow! This is how me and Bo is gonna be living soon," Donna said.

"Shut up! Where are the others, pal, and what's beyond that door?" Sully asked Cal.

"Just beyond is a group of regular airline seats. Five rows, I think. Beyond that is another door leading to the cargo area. I'm not sure where they are," Cal answered.

"Call them."

Again, Cal hesitated.

"Look, easy or hard, I don't need them. I can just send Larry in there blasting, and we won't have to worry about them. Or, you can call them," Sully warned.

Cal knew from experience when an enemy was bluffing, and this man's eyes told him that he meant what he said.

"Jan, grab Amy and Chris and come in here, will you?" Cal yelled.

"Can't it wait? We are almost done here," came Jan's reply from the back of the plane.

It killed him to hear her voice and have to call her again.

"No, we need to go over this now."

"All right, we'll be right there."

A few seconds later, the door opened and Chris Mitchell stepped through, followed by his wife and mother.

"What's so important tha..." Chris stopped in mid-sentence. "Dad, what's going on?"

Cal looked from his son to his daughter-in-law to his wife, seeing combined looks of surprise, confusion, and fear. All three were staring at him for answers.

"Welcome to the party. Dad has been kind enough to invite us to join you good people on this flight, and we have accepted. Now take a seat on the couch and don't move. I've already told the old man that if you cooperate no one will get hurt," Sully said.

"Cal, what's he talking about?" Jan asked.

"Let's just do what he says kiddo, okay?" Cal said, guiding them toward the couch.

"Cal. Good, that makes it easier to communicate, and you would be smart to just sit there and do as I say," Sully said. Then, turning to the others, he started barking out orders.

"Caitlin, go get Jimmy and have him bring in the bags."

"Larry, check out the rest of this rig. Be careful just in case our buddy, Cal, was lying about how many passengers we've got on board."

"Donna, find out from Bo how long before this tub takes off."

All three moved at once, leaving the Mitchell family staring at Mike Sullivan, wondering what was in store for them next.

*   *   *   *   *

Jimmy Kann was not happy as he dragged the first bag through the curtain into the living quarters of the plane.

'Hey! Could I get some help, Sully?" he asked, as he dropped the bag on the floor. Kann was still complaining when Larry Webster returned from his search of the plane.

"Everything's as they said, Sully. No one else on board. There's a cargo door out back where we can throw our stuff."

"Okay, you guys get the rest of our stuff stowed away and see if you can find some rope while you're out there. The young guy here will be glad to help. Won't you, kid?" Sully said.

Chris looked to Cal who answered for him.

"Go on, Chris. Amy will be fine here with us."

Chris and Webster moved toward the door, but Kann was blocking their path. He had not moved. He spotted Jan and Amy, and he liked what he was seeing. This was an added bonus. The thrill of the job and the money were important, but a couple of good looking broads would be icing on the cake. He just had to convince Sully to let him at them. He never could understand Sully when it came to women. For Kann the thrill was not just in the sex, but in the pain and humiliation he could inflict.

Sully gave him a shove.

"Hey Jimmy, am I speaking a foreign language here? Get your ass moving."

As he turned to go, Kann looked back with a grin that sent chills down the spine of both Jan and Amy.

Cal stared at the floor. He had not missed the grin.

*   *   *   *   *

Kann was still smiling as he passed the rest of the gear up into the cargo hold. All he could think of were the women on board and where he could get a chance at them.

The young one was smaller, maybe 5'5", slightly buil,t with long, blond hair and a beautiful face. She would be fun, he thought, but the other one really turned him on. She was quite a bit older than him, but boy, was she put together.

Jan Mitchell turned men's heads whether she wore jeans or an evening dress. Tall, at 5' 10", and 130 pounds, she really did look closer to thirty-five than fifty. She had shiny, shoulder length auburn hair and kept in shape playing racquetball and working out daily at her health club.

Her great shape did not go unnoticed by Kann, and that's why he was smiling when Webster yelled down at him from the cargo hold door.

"Hey, let's go! Quit daydreaming. Sully's gonna kill us if we don't hurry."

"Keep your pants on. Here's the last bag." Kann said as he hoisted up the black golf bag. "Close up here. I'm going back in the side door."

Inside, Donna explained to Sully what would happen at takeoff. A ground crew would be summoned to tow them from the hangar to the tarmac. There, they would start the engines and taxi to the runway. Until then Bo would remain up front with the pilot.

Caitlin and Kann entered from the front passageway as Webster pushed Chris into the room from the back of the plane. Webster held the Bizon in one hand and a coil of rope in the other.

"All right, Larry, take the kids next door and tie them up. Leave them in the seats. Hands in front, no gags. It will stay that way as long as we don't get any trouble. Any funny stuff and we will throw the four of you out back trussed up like cattle. Do you understand?" Sully looked directly at Cal as he spoke.

24

"We understand. Chris and Amy, do as he says. It will be all right."

Chris led Amy into the middle portion of the plane, followed by Webster. Kann was visibly upset. He would have liked to tie up the little blonde himself.

"You two will stay here for awhile," Sullivan said. "We may need you for information on the plane or where we are going. We still have three hours to go before we leave, and I don't want any heroics, so I'm keeping her here in case you get any crazy ideas." he said, looking directly at Cal.

"Just exactly what do you want? Why not just take the plane or at least let them go," Jan demanded, motioning toward the door where Chris and Amy had disappeared.

Sully's eyes narrowed. "I've had enough things go wrong today. Don't make me gag you, lady. Jimmy, close that door and let's all relax. We're going to be together for awhile."

Instead of doing what he was told, Kann put his hand on Sully's shoulder and said with a laugh, "What do you say I take her out back and keep her busy for awhile. I bet she'll be quiet after I'm done with her."

Sully turned until he was close enough to Kann that they could feel each other's breath. When he spoke, Cal and Jan could barely hear him.

"Jimmy, you go close that door and stay where I can see you for the rest of this trip. Stay away from them. You're not screwing this deal up for me, you sick bastard. Do you understand?"

Kann was bigger and stronger than Sully, but he didn't hesitate this time. As he left, Sully turned to his sister. "Caitlin, where's that cell-phone?"

Caitlin sat on the edge of a recliner. She sat with her elbows on her knees, rubbing her temples with both hands. She didn't hear the question. She was as frightened as she had ever been in her life. Nothing had gone right, and if her brother found out that she was the one who ratted him out, she would be dead.

They had never been close. From as far back as she could remember, she had been scared of him, and it wouldn't be the first time he hurt her.

During her brother's last stint in Rikers, she decided to get away form him and straighten out her life. She moved from the city to Long Island and got a job at a King Kullen supermarket. She steadily moved up to deli manager and was currently dating the assistant manager of the store. He knew nothing of her past, and she wanted it to stay that way.

Everything was going great until Sully called. She tried to beg off, but he made it clear. He wasn't asking. He was telling. Caitlin knew if he was convicted, he would never be paroled again, but she didn't care. All she wanted was to be left alone. Caitlin called N.Y.P.D. and asked for Detective Martini.

"Caitlin, did you hear me? What the hell is wrong with you? Where is the damn phone?" Sully yelled.

Caitlin jumped up and grabbed her handbag. "Right here, Sully."

Sully took the phone and stared at his sister for a long time. Finally, he looked at his watch. It was 12:30 P.M. Eastern Standard Time; it would be 2:20 in New Mexico. What difference did it make? They were going to be two days earlier than expected. That's if his new plan worked and they made it to Las Cruces.

Chapter 9

Traci Leigh Bradley! Mrs. James Bradley! Unbelievable, Traci thought, as she finished writing the last payroll check.

Okay, I'm done. The school is set for the next ten days, during which time I'll be married and then headed for The Cayman Islands. Sun, food, drink, relaxation, and Jimmy. What could be better?

Back to reality. Francine would be in charge, no problem there. She had been with Traci for five years and knew the business inside and out. Traci would have her pager and cell-phone, but it would take a real emergency for Francine to call.

Her main reason for coming in today was to do the payroll for the next two weeks and to kill the morning so she wouldn't go crazy. She had accomplished both, and now she could put the finishing touches on the wedding.

Traci Mitchell was twenty-eight—strikingly beautiful with long, red hair and dark green eyes. She was tall like her mother and slender, almost on the slim side. Actually, she was thinner than usual, thanks to her self-imposed three month fast, designed to fit her perfectly into her wedding dress.

Traci opened her daily planner to check the wedding list.

The Bradleys, Jim's parents, had set the rehearsal dinner for 7:00 P.M. tonight at Carmine's Restaurant. Jim called to say that the rest of his family had arrived, and he and his brother, Tim, were leaving to get the tuxedos. She told him there was nothing else for him to do and she would swing by to pick him up later so they could go get her parents at the airport. I wish I could say there was nothing else for me to do, she thought. Let's see. Dress fitting today, check...photographer, yes... limo, taken care of...cake, all set... band, got it...flowers, bouquet, boutonnieres, church, reception, set...Holiday Inn. Joni, the banquet manager, was taking care of everything there from flowers to food. Good! That's everything. Everything, that is, except me. Where did I put my other list?

TO DO

Today

Pick up Michelle and Kerry at 2:00.
Holiday Inn
            (See Linda, check with Joni)

                Final fitting 2:30 at JASMINE'S
Meet Mom & Dad at airport 5:30
Rehearsal 6:30
Dinner CARMINE'S 7:00
Jimmy, alone, sometime tonight?
Pack.
Have a drink.
Sleep. (yeah, right)!

Tomorrow

EAT SOMETHING, FORCE YOURSELF!!
8:00 hair STEFFI'S
9:00 dress
9:30 pictures
10:30 limo
11:00 wedding
11:35 married. Yikes!!!
12:00 party!!!

Traci closed her notebook and glanced at her watch. 1:00 P.M. She still had an hour, she thought. She leaned back in her chair and closed her eyes. *I never thought this would happen after Barry. I never thought I would be happy again.*

She had met Barry Rider during her freshman year at Georgetown University. He was in pre-law, and she fell in love. They lived together for three years, and she assumed they would be together forever. He had other plans. On the day he passed the bar, he informed her as he packed that there had been no promises. It had been fun, but he was moving on alone.

Traci was crushed. Cal wanted her to come home for a semester, but she didn't want to answer questions or deal with the pity of her family. She stayed at Georgetown that summer working in a daycare center and vowing never to be hurt again.

She moved to Tucson after graduation and started her own school. TRACI'S KIDS, located in a large, ranch style house on the outskirts of town, specialized in a program of intervention. Intervention allowed exceptional children and children with special needs to be entered in classes with mainstream students, working and learning together. The school started out with an infant room, a toddler's room, and a nursery school and filled to capacity within three months of its opening. Four years later, pressure from parents whose children were moving on prompted her to expand the school to include its own kindergarten. As fate would have it, she hired Jim Bradley and his construction crew to do the renovations.

Jim Bradley worked for her for three weeks. One morning after reviewing the school's blueprints with her, he asked her to go bowling. She had never been bowling in her life but found herself saying yes anyway. She still wasn't keen on bowling, but she enjoyed his company enough that she agreed to see him again the next night. It wasn't long before she fell in love with the handsome, rugged, manual laborer.

Traci opened her eyes and breathed deeply.

"God, I love you," she said to the picture of Jim on her desk. "1:20! I'm out of here. More time to visit with Linda." She pressed the intercom button.

"Fran, I'm out of here. I'll see you tonight."

"Can't wait. Call me if you need anything last minute," came the reply.

"Thanks, I will."

Traci slung her bag over her shoulder, turned out the lights, and closed the door behind her.

Chapter 10

Thursday, just seven days before The Grand National opening, The *Circle R* stock was being loaded on trucks that would soon leave for a two day trip to the coast. The ranch supplied livestock for most of the top rodeos in the United States and Canada. Starting in January with the Western Stock Show and Rodeo in Denver, Colorado, they worked almost every event right up to Nationals at the Cow Palace in Las Vegas.

Rory took Carrie to her first show at The Grand National Finals. By the end of the week, she was hooked. From the Las Vegas strip to the competition itself, there was a feeling of excitement. She soon learned that rodeo people were family, helping out and rooting for each other no matter how tense the competition got. The *Circle R* crew handled their own stock and helped out in the chutes with the other animals. Everyone knew Rory even though he had retired from calf roping ten years earlier. He still held most of the career records and was liked and respected by everyone.

Carrie had been around athletes her whole life, but what these men and women did with their bodies simply amazed her.

She watched men limp from the arena to the medical tent only to find they had broken bones. She saw men with broken cheekbones, noses, or jaws, men bleeding from cuts and gashes. They wore casts and went so far as to have an arm strapped to their side to go on to the next round. For the top ten cowboys the money could be pretty good, but it was a hell of a way to make a living.

The show started with the women in the barrel races. She marveled at the speed and grace the cowgirls used to guide their mounts through the obstacles. It was enough to tell her that she wanted to learn to ride like them.

The precision between two cowboys and their respective mounts during the calf roping left her in awe. She watched as men dropped from horses at full speed onto the horns of a moving steer in the steer wrestling competition. She wondered how any of the men participating in the bronco busting—either saddle or bareback—could walk the next day, no less get on and ride again.

But what defined the rodeo for Carrie were the bull riders. As rugged as they were, these men were not very big in stature. Yet,time after time, they climbed on the back of an enraged animal weighing close to a thousand pounds whose intent was not just to buck them off, but to kill them if given the chance. All of this for eight seconds of glory.

The only people at the rodeo crazier than the bull riders, in her opinion, were the bullfighters. They actually stood in the ring and enticed the bull to come after them to protect the rider. They dressed as clowns, but their jobs were more serious than any other at the rodeo.

When they returned to the ranch, Carrie couldn't wait to learn all there was to know about the business of the *Circle R*. She never dreamed when he taught her how to ride, how to shoot, and how to run the ranch that she would ever have to use that knowledge to carry on without him.

Rory had a tradition of taking the month of December off so everyone could be with his or her family through the holidays, and Carrie had kept that tradition alive. The crew were grateful for the time off, but Carrie hated this time of year. Two more shows after the Nationals and the ranch would be virtually deserted except for a skeleton crew. When the ranch shut down there wasn't much to do except feed and water the stock and retool the equipment.

Carrie went back east for Thanksgiving and Christmas the first two years after Rory's death. It had been so awkward being there alone with everyone asking how she was doing. Was she seeing anyone and how sorry they felt for her. She knew they meant well, but it just made things worse. Since then, she spent this time of year tying up loose ends on the ranch, from paper work to checking equipment to general repairs.

It was a long way from Caroline Martin of Cortland, New York, to Carrie Douglas of Midland, Texas. Rory had called her Carrie from the moment they met. She couldn't remember the last person outside of Cortland who had called her Caroline.

Back home Carrie had been one of the best athletes in the state, but she did not know what being in condition was until she married Rory. That first year it seemed as if every muscle in her body was sore on a regular basis. Now she did not have an ounce of fat on her anywhere. She was a dark tan with golden hair, which was almost always kept in a French braid under one of her ten-gallon hats. She worked regularly with the crew which kept her 5'6", 115 pound frame in excellent condition.

It was hard for any man not to notice Carrie Douglas.

She was a different person now, and Cortland was another lifetime, she thought, as she filled in the last entry on the inventory form.

"Here you go, Brett, you know the drill as well as I do. Have a safe trip and call me when you get there, and again after you meet with Rodgers."

"Sure you don't want to come along ma'am? I know you love the competition," Brett offered.

"It's foolish, I know, but not this one,Brett, not this one."

"Okay, then we're outta here. I'll call from Frisco."

"Okay. I've got plenty to do here until then. I'm going to relax. Take a hot bath for an hour, heat up a big bowl of beef stew, open up a bottle of cabernet and do nothing but laze around 'til you guys return. Maybe if I get some ambition late next week, I'll start thinking about our next gig in Missouri."

Brett tipped his hat and climbed up into the big rig. As they drove off, he looked in the side mirror at Carrie Douglas watching them drive away. She looked small and vulnerable, much different from the strong, competent owner of the *Circle R* that he knew her to be. When his long-time boss and friend first told him about the city girl he was going to marry, Brett had been more than a little skeptical. Now, seventeen years later, he marveled at how tough and capable his new boss had become. He only wished she could be happy again.

Chapter 11

The long-term parking lot at MacArthur was close to full when Skip Amanski and his son, Ben, arrived. They had twenty minutes to catch the 4:30 flight on Southwest Airlines to Tucson, Arizona. Ben's game had gone into overtime, and the traffic from Southampton had been brutal.

Ben was a star fullback and linebacker on the Southampton football team. The team was 6-0, and Ben had already rushed for over eight hundred yards and scored twelve touchdowns, including the game winner today.

Colleges were lining up to talk to him even though he was only a junior. At 6'3", 225 pounds, with a 3.5 grade point average, it seemed he would have quite a few choices before all was said and done. Skip arranged for all inquiries to go through the school athletic department. They were instructed to inform all those interested that the Amanski family would not entertain any offers before his senior season ended.

The rest of the Amanski clan, Skip's wife, Linda, and daughters had left the night before. Michelle was a bridesmaid, and Traci wanted her there as early as possible. Skip smiled as he parked the car, thinking how great it was that Cal's kids and his kids had always been so close. It obviously started with the relationship between Cal and Skip, but over the years, their wives also became very close. Cal and Jan served as godparents to Kerry—Skip and Linda's youngest—and the children spent so much time together growing up that they all seemed like brothers and sisters rather than friends. He remembered clearly the day it all started.

Like his son, Skip was a star athlete and student in high school. He was pursuing a degree in criminology at Duke University when a man named Richard Ireland first contacted him. The pitch had been good, and the agency would pay for the rest of his schooling, including graduate school. The assignments would take him around the world. After a year, if he wanted out, they would place him anywhere he wanted to go in the law enforcement field. He quickly found out that Richard Ireland almost always got what he wanted.

Within hours, he persuaded Skip to join an organization that he never even considered as a job option. Skip partnered with Cal from the first day, and it had been a defining moment for both of their lives. They worked as partners for two years all over the world; in countries friendly to the United States and those that were not. Their work took them from the underbelly of drug trafficking to the high stakes business of counter-espionage. They were in many tight spots, always watching each other's back, and they walked away from places they could not have gotten out of alone. All of this under the watchful eyes of Ireland.

Behind the scenes in Washington, D.C., Richard Ireland was a very powerful man. The Director and Assistant Director of the CIA stood before the cameras and answered questions, but Ireland got things done.

After two years, Skip and Cal left the agency and started to build SKIPCAL into a Wall Street giant. What started out as a temporary partnership ended up as a lifetime friendship. Skip wondered if he would be more excited if one of his own children were getting married.

"Let's go, B.J. Looks like we're going to have to run for it. I guess you didn't get enough exercise today," he said, as he grabbed his bag and slammed the door.

Ben had his duffel bag slung over his shoulder and was already jogging toward the terminal. He looked back and laughed.

"I'm just worried about having to carry you," he shouted.

Skip was the same height as his son and ten pounds heavier, but that's where the similarities ended. Where Ben had a full head of close-cropped dark brown hair and a clean-shaven face, his dad was pretty much bald with salt and pepper hair on the sides and a mustache of the same color.

Skip grinned and started after Ben. He was looking forward to this weekend. Of course, the marriage of his godchild would be the big event. However, he would be lying if he said he wasn't almost as excited about the two tee times he and Cal had with their sons for Sunday and Monday mornings.

The four of them hardly ever got to play together anymore. If Cal was right, this would be a big challenge. Supposedly, Chris was now an eight handicap, and Ben shot in the mid-forties every time he played. This could cost them some money at a buck a hole.

They arrived at the gate just in time to hear the final boarding call. Being in first class did not save them from the icy look they got from the woman checking passes. They hurried down the tunnel to start what was to be a weekend of fun and games in the Arizona desert.

Chapter 12

Detective Frank Martini looked at his watch one more time. It was now 5:30 in the evening, seven and a half hours after Sullivan and his people met the plane from South America. The airport search started an hour later and turned up nothing. They posted men at every entrance to the terminal and alerted the people watching the airlines. He sent his men to check ground transportation, and they conducted a canvas of every parking garage. Finally, they spread out and checked every gate, restaurant, bar, and restroom. None of their interviews had turned up anything. No one remembered seeing them.

Damn, he thought, how could they just disappear? All check points had called in twice, and he kept them at least an hour after he knew it was hopeless. They had escaped. But how? It would haunt him until he knew the answer. If he ever did. Martini glanced back at the terminal as he ducked his head and entered the unmarked car that would take him back to the precinct.

He felt they had covered all the bases on this one, complete with issuing an all-points bulletin. The bosses had listened to his description of the anonymous phone call and had gone along with him. He would have to face the music when he returned. Well, it wouldn't be the first or last time some desk jockey criticized his police work.

What galled him was that the informant had been correct. Sullivan was there, and the group had picked up the bags. They had gone to the elevators. Why they didn't get on, he would probably never know. Bottom line—he let them escape.

He slammed his fist on the dashboard.

"Goddamn it! Where the hell did they go?"

Chapter 13

The buildings on the *Circle R* were spread out across a large complex with the main barn, stockades, and stables on the western edge of the open expanse. To the right of the stables were the bunkhouses used for temporary workers. On the other side, a hundred yards away, stood the residences of the workers who lived on the ranch full time. The main ranch house was located directly across from the barn.

The *Circle R* supplied an assortment of stock for the rodeos along with handling quarter horses, which were for sale or used for work on the ranch. Interested wranglers came to the ranch on certain weekends to watch the herd for a horse that might catch their eye. The price of a quality quarter horse is steep, but the horse is the cowboy's most essential possession, and the *Circle R*'s reputation was unparalleled in the business. The ranch also kept a herd of cattle for onsite calf roping, steer wrestling, and for feeding the crew. Just like farm life, the work on a ranch never seemed to end.

Carrie sat on the porch swing drinking an ice cold Heineken. It was 3:30 P.M., Central Standard Time. She and those left on the ranch had been working straight out since the others left. Carrie told them when everything was caught up they were free for the night. It was amazing what could be accomplished with a goal like that in front of you. She drained her beer and headed inside.

Upstairs, the whirlpool bath was nearly full with steaming hot water. The smell of lilacs filled her senses as she reached to shut off the faucet. As Carrie removed her bathrobe and hung it on the back of the door, she looked at her reflection in the full-length mirror. Not bad, she thought, still in pretty good shape.

It had been a long time since any man had seen or touched her in this condition. Sad, but true, she thought. Her hormones had certainly not disappeared, and she had had several chances to act on them, mostly at rodeos and conventions she had attended. Once, not long ago, she came close.

She went to dinner with him and had a great time. She danced with him, slowly, letting him guide her with his hands and body. He kissed her, and she kissed him back. But when he wanted to lead her to his room, she backed out at the last minute. She just couldn't go through with it as much as her body told her to. Was it too soon—or fear that expectations would not be reached? Questions she still did not know the answers to.

She shook her head and climbed into the tub. Those thoughts were not going to help her relax, and that was all she wanted tonight. The hot water washed over her body as she reached for a glass of wine on the marble ledge.

"God, this feels good," she sighed.

Chapter 14

When Bo first entered the cockpit, he held his index finger to his lips, signaling silence, which he reinforced by the gun he pointed at the pilot's head. The stunned look on Billy Cannon's face told Bo that he would not be saying anything soon. Quickly he took the pad of paper and pencil he had under his arm and started writing:

> *Do not speak. Do not make any false moves. My friends have taken over this plane, and we are going to fly out of here on schedule. I can fly this plane, so we can do this with or without you. First, I want to know if the flight recorders have been turned on.*

As the initial shock wore off, Billy took the pad from Bo and began to write. *The recorders come on automatically when the engines start, but they can be shut on and off manually.*

"Good! From now on, you do as I say until we are in the air and out of range of the New York radar. I will hear every word you say when you talk to the controllers in the tower. Do not make any mistakes, and we will get along fine. Do you understand?" Bo said.

In a halting voice, Billy managed to answer, "I understand. Just take it easy with that gun."

*   *   *   *   *

The plane got off the ground without a hitch, and Bo continued to communicate with Billy by written word. They followed the original flight plan and were on a path set for Tucson, Arizona.

Before they left the ground, Sully contacted Richie Gomez in Las Cruces. As soon as he got on the phone, Gomez started talking.

"Sully, did you get the stuff?"

"Yeah, I got the stuff. Now, shut up and listen. The plans have changed. I need to talk to Escalia."

"I don't know, Sully. He's not going to like this. What kind of changes do you mean?"

"I don't care what you like, Richie. Get Escalia on the phone."

"He ain't here. I'll get him and have him call you back. What's your number?"

"555-7809. Make it quick, Richie. I could sell this stuff to anyone," Sully said, just before he disconnected the call.

He had no intention of dealing any further with the Gomez brothers. Juan Escalia was the head of all drug trafficking in southern New Mexico, and he could get whatever he wanted. To make this deal work, he would need Escalia's help. They were now two hours into the flight, and Sully was getting edgy. They had to make a move soon, and he knew it. Just then, the phone in his hand rang.

"Yeah?" This is Sullivan. Who am I talking to?"

"I am Juan Escalia. Your friend tells me that you have my merchandise, but there is a problem."

"We had some bad luck, but we took care of it. The problem is we are on a plane instead of in a van. Also, we will be arriving in two hours instead of two days. We need a place to land, transportation out of there, and the money."

It was a few minutes before Escalia answered. "This is very short notice, but we have a private landing strip that we use, and the transportation you originally requested has already been taken care of. As for the money, I don't think that will be a problem."

"Good. There was nothing we could do about the timing of this, but the good news is that we have your packages. I will put my man on for the directions on where to land. We will be there in a couple of hours, and we can close this deal," Sully said.

"I will look forward to seeing you. Be careful, amigo. Miguel will speak to your friend. Adios."

Twenty minutes later, Bo got off the line. He explained that he had the coordinates to Escalia's private landing strip. He told Sully he would have to change course and drop to a lower altitude. He was pretty certain they had not been picked up on radar. The Tucson Airport had not contacted them since they left New York. Within the hour, Bo dropped the plane to fifteen thousand feet and found a direct path to Las Cruces.

Sully had no more use for the Mitchell family or Billy Cannon, and he did not like loose ends. It was time to get them out of the way.

"Larry, Jimmy, put the two young ones in the cargo hold, tie their feet, and gag them."

"Come on! We've done everything you've asked," Jan said. "This isn't necessary, we aren't going anywhere," she yelled, as the two men left to carry out Sully's order.

"No, it's not necessary, but I'll feel better, and that's all that matters," Sully replied. "Okay, let's go. You guys are going out back with the other two."

The group headed toward the back of the plane, led by Cal, who continued to watch and wait for an opening to try to turn the tables on their captors. He had to admire the way Sully split them up from the beginning. It made it close to impossible to overtake one man without putting other members of his family in even more danger.

When they reached the door to the cargo hold, Jimmy Kann was waiting. "Larry's finishing up with the kid. The girl was easy and fun," he grinned.

"Good. Take one of these three next—I'll watch the others," Sully told him.

Jimmy Kann had never been a very lucky guy, and this moment was no exception. Jan Mitchell was the closest person to him. "My pleasure!" he said.

That was the last thing he ever said. Jan was wearing faded blue jeans and a waist length sweater vest. Kann grabbed her from behind, with one arm going across her chest just under her neck, while the other hand snaked up under the vest, ripped her bra, and painfully grabbed her left breast. Cal had been trained to protect himself and others in many different ways, and he always thought out whatever action he took; even as an agent when situations called for quick and deadly force. He had never seen the woman he loved manhandled this way. He reacted with a vengeance and speed that belied his age and size.

Jimmy Kann never knew he screamed in agony from the kick that crashed into the side of his left knee, tearing all three ligaments and dislocating the kneecap. As he let go his grasp to look down at his destroyed leg, his head was grabbed in a vice-like grip. He never felt the sharp twist that broke his neck, killing him instantly.

Jan and Billy stared at Cal in disbelief. A man they had known for years had just killed someone. Neither of them would have believed him capable of such an act, but they had seen it with their own eyes.

Mike Sullivan saw it too, and though he couldn't care less about the life of Jimmy Kann, he cared very much how he died.

Sully had seen some dangerous men in his time, but he had never seen anyone put out of commission that fast and effectively. Their eyes locked, and Sully knew he was looking at pure danger in this man. At that same instant, Cal knew there was nowhere to run.

He turned to look at Jan as Sullivan raised the Magnum and fired twice. The first bullet struck his upper right chest and the second hit the left side of his head as the power of the first shot turned his body right and downward. He felt a blinding pain in his head and heard Jan scream, "No!"

Cal fell lifeless through the door into the cargo area.

Chapter 15

Skip couldn't concentrate. He closed his book and sat back in his chair. They had been the last passengers to board, and the plane started to taxi as soon as they were strapped in. He glanced at Ben sleeping next to him. Skip never slept more than six hours a night and never failed to let Ben know how jealous he was of his son's ability to sleep anywhere at anytime. Of course, Linda always reminded him that he couldn't sleep because he drank too much coffee and soda.

His thoughts drifted to his best friend, Cal, and he started smiling. He had seen Cal in every kind of situation over the years, and he had always been the calmest, most levelheaded guy around. Well, he had a feeling that would change around eleven o'clock on Saturday when Cal started down the aisle to give Traci away. He was going to enjoy watching Cal sweat for once. Skip wanted badly to rub it in, but he had to be careful. He knew his time would come when Michelle and Kerry would get married. That was not going to happen in the near future. For now, he would rub it in gleefully.

His daughters were twenty and fourteen respectively, and neither one had a steady boyfriend. Michelle had broken it off with the guy she dated for awhile at Penn State, and Kerry was too young. At least, that was what he had told Kerry during their latest argument. Skip wondered if all fathers fought more with their daughters than with their sons? He and Kerry seemed to argue more and more these days, and he hated it, but he was not going to let her fall by the wayside because he wasn't paying attention. As usual, Linda stepped into the latest episode before it got nasty saying, "I'll talk to your dad about this later."

Great! Well, he was not giving in on this one. It was bad enough that she was going to the freshman dances. She would not be going steady before her sophomore year. Ben had a steady string of girls after him, and he always had a date, but even he wasn't going steady. With Ben it was different. He was a guy. Whoa! Better not let that slip, or the whole female family contingent would be on his back.

Jeez, it sucks being a parent sometimes, especially when your youngest daughter reaches puberty, he thought. Where the hell was I and how did I get so far off track?

He let his mind drift back to the weekend. Best friends, family, fun, and golf. He laughed and closed his eyes. This was going to be a great weekend.

Chapter 16

Back in New York City, at the 37th Precinct, Detective Martini was fuming. After an hour in Captain Strong's office listening to a litany of bureaucratic mumbo jumbo about how operations like his wasted the taxpayers' money, he was ready to explode. Strong made it clear to him that the Captain would catch it from the chief, who would catch from the commissioner who, in turn, would have to answer to the mayor. It was amazing to him how these guys changed as soon as they got a new title.

Captain Strong was one of the best cops he had ever worked with, but after three years on a desk, he seemed to have forgotten everything about what could go wrong on the street. During the conference call with city hall, not once did he defend Martini's actions. Instead, after hanging up, he blasted Martini and warned of possible suspensions. He was not going to jeopardize his own job to protect someone else. If the big bosses went after Martini's shield, he would be on his own.

Idiots! Not one of them could see the reality of what happened. Yes, somehow he let them escape, but the fact remained that his tip was correct. Sullivan's group had been at the airport. They were at the baggage claim carousel. They picked up the bags. You would have to be a fool not to believe the rest of the story from Caitlin Sullivan. A large amount of cocaine had just entered the city. That was the clear fact that needed to be addressed.

Collins identified Mike and Caitlin Sullivan along with Robert "Bo" Boston right away. Martini's people were already going over their files, and Collins was working with a police artist on composites for the other three gang members. All precincts, along with drug enforcement personnel, were told to be on the lookout for an influx of cocaine and any sign of Mike Sullivan or his group.

Martini sat back and took a long drag from his cigarette. I've gotta give these up, he thought for the hundredth time. What had started out as a promising day for Detective Martini had gone sou,r and it did not look as if it was going to improve anytime soon.

Chapter 17

On board the 727, chaos reigned. When the shots rang out and Cal fell through the cargo door, Larry Webster almost shot him again. He had just finished tying Chris's feet and whirled to a firing position on his knees, pointing at the fallen man's head.

"Sully! What the hell's going on?" he yelled. Just then, Jan burst through the door, falling at Cal's side screaming.

"Cal! Cal! Oh, my God, Cal, don't die!"

Chris could only see one side of his father's face, and it was covered with blood. He tried to rip free of the ropes, but there was no way. Tears streamed down his face. He never felt so helpless in his life.

In the forward room, Sully pointed the gun at Billy's head.

"If you want to live, get in the back room now and drag his sorry ass in there with you," he said, motioning to Kann's lifeless body.

Billy pulled the body into the cargo hold followed quickly by Mike Sullivan. Jan was frantically trying to stop her husband's bleeding with her hands and begging him to stay alive. Too late for that, sister, he thought. He should have kept his cool.

"What happened to Jimmy?" Larry wanted to know.

"Our hero here didn't like Jimmy grabbing his old lady, so he snapped Jimmy's neck. Well, that pissed me off, so I shot him, and I'm going to keep shooting people if I get anymore trouble on this plane. Do you understand?" Sully yelled. "Larry, drag our stuff out of here and lock them in. We'll deal with them after we land. Don't get all worked up about Kann. It just means more money for us."

As soon as the lock clicked on the door, Jan's manner changed dramatically from hysterical wife to a person in control. "Billy, quick, untie them," she said, feeling for a pulse in Cal's neck. Jan prayed she could remember enough first aid to save her husband's life.

"Cal, can you hear me? Squeeze my hand if you can."

"Ma, is he alive?" Chris yelled, as he ripped the gag from his mouth.

"Barely. I found a pulse, but it's very weak. Go get the first aid kit and grab some towels from that old trunk out back. Quickly! We have to stop the bleeding if we can."

As she spoke, her eyes darted around the cargo hold searching for something—an answer—a way out. They stopped on the emergency door handle to the right of the cargo door. Instantly she made up her mind. She looked up at Chris who had returned with the towels.

"Grab five parachutes from under the shelf at the back of the plane. Get the ski jackets, too. Amy, help him. Quickly!"

"Mom, what are you saying?" Chris asked.

"We're getting out of here. If we stay here, they will kill us sooner or later. That man shot your father like it meant nothing to him. When this plane lands, he is not going to let us walk away, and he's not about to get a doctor for your dad."

Amy's face was white as she looked from Jan to Chris. "I can't! I've never done it! I wouldn't know what to do!" she cried.

"Mom, she's right. It's been years since Dad made us take those lessons. I'm not sure I remember what to do myself," Chris said.

"Just get the damn chutes, Chris, and don't argue with me. We don't have a choice," Jan shouted.

Chris had never seen a more determined look in his mother's eyes. "Okay," he said, and headed for the rear of the plane.

Minutes later, all four were strapped into harnesses, and Billy was giving a refresher course to Chris with Amy looking on anxiously.

Jan tied a tight bandage around Cal's head. She found an entry wound in his chest and an exit wound in his back and covered both with clean rags and gauze. She then wrapped towels around his upper chest to help stem the bleeding. Next, she put Cal in a ski jacket and hooked him into his chute. Then, she carefully began to unravel it from the knapsack.

"Why are you letting it out now?" Amy asked.

"When we jump, I will hang on to Cal if I can, but if I can't, I want to make sure his chute is open. I'll take your dad first. Then, Chris with Amy—and then Billy. Remember. Get free of the plane before you pull the cord. Try to keep each other in sight. If not, get help as fast as possible." She paused for a moment and touched Cal's cheek.

Quickly refocusing her attention, she spoke. "Billy, hang onto Cal while I pull this lever down. Everyone else hold on to something solid. They never pressurized the cabin, so that shouldn't be a problem, but who knows how the plane will react. It will be extremely cold, and the wind will be fierce. Everyone all set? Here goes." She grabbed the handle and pulled down with all of her strength.

Sully had just started on his second beer when the plane gave a sudden jolt. Before he could react, Donna burst through the cockpit door.

"Hey! Bo says the cargo door just opened."

Sully was on his feet running for the back of the plane in an instant, with Larry close behind.

Jan managed to slide Cal to the edge of the doorway despite the howling wind whipping into the plane. She decided to push him to the rim and let his body weight carry her out as he dropped over the edge. She had maneuvered them to that position when Amy's scream made her look back.

Sully stood holding Amy with his gun pressed to the side of her head. "Get up and move away from that door if you want them to live," Sully yelled.

She knew they could just roll and be out of this, drifting through the sky. She knew that Cal had no chance of living on the plane and probably little more if he got off, but at least he would have a chance. There was no way that she could leave Chris and Amy behind.

Jan leaned close and whispered in Cal's ear, "Live, baby. Just live!" She then let go and stood up. As she did, Cal dropped through the open doorway and disappeared from sight.

Sully rushed to the door but was too late to see what happened to the man he shot. The ground below was a mixture of wide open spaces and mountain terrain.

His mind was racing. The chances were good that the son of a bitch wouldn't land near a town. The problem was, even though he was most certainly dead, sooner or later someone might find him. Sully hated to be outsmarted. He hated loose ends, and right now, he really hated the whole Mitchell family. He wanted to finish them now, but he had to control himself. Shooting them now did not fit into his plans. He had already acted without thinking once, and he wasn't about to do it again. He stepped back and stared at Jan Mitchell for a moment.

"That was stupid," he shouted. "He'll be dead before he hits the ground if he isn't dead already."

Jan said nothing. The look of hatred was unmistakable. He knew then that she was as dangerous as her husband. Their eyes never wavered from each other as Sully spoke. "Larry, I'll cover you while you tie and gag them. Then find out how to close this door. They'll stay here for the rest of the trip."

Chapter 18

Traci arrived at the hotel early. She couldn't wait to fill Linda in on all of the plans for the next two days. Traci knew that Linda and her mom talked every day about the wedding, but it would still be fun to go over it with the woman who had been like a second mother to her. Besides, one last time over her checklist couldn't hurt.

Traci, Michelle, and Kerry arrived fifteen minutes late for their fittings at Jasmine's, but it wasn't busy, and they got right in. Michelle looked beautiful in her navy blue bridesmaid dress. The pleated gown flowed to the floor from a gathered waist. The bodice had a slightly plunging neckline with spaghetti straps and an open back to the waistline. Though her measurements were given over the phone, with a few pins and tucks, it was a perfect fit.

Traci's dress was a soft strapless gown with a medium train and a scalloped front. The white gown, small headpiece, and veil all stood out in contrast to her red hair and dark tan. Traci looked radiant. Just for fun, the three girls tried on a half dozen dresses each before they left.

Instead of going back to the hotel for lunch, they decided to kill two birds with one stone. Traci wanted to do a final run-through on the reception with Joni, so they decided to get a bite to eat and a few drinks at Carmine's. They had a ball reminiscing and chatting about the upcoming events, but in the process, Traci lost track of time.

She glanced at her watch as she pushed her Lexus through rush hour traffic. She left the girls at the hotel and was trying to get to Jim's as fast as possible. She knew he would be waiting. He always teased her about being late, and this would be no different. She told him she would be there by four, but it was already five past, and she was still ten minutes away.

They had wanted to get to the airport early to relax and spend a little time together. With everything so hectic, it had been awhile since they were able to just sit and talk.

Traci smiled, remembering the last visit from her family. In April, Dad, Mom, and Uncle Skip came out for a golf weekend. Mom played once and then spent the rest of her time with Traci planning the wedding. All the preparations since had been handled by phone. On top of that, she hadn't seen Chris and Amy since their wedding a year ago last August.

Traci and Chris were as close as any brother and sister could be. In the early years, Traci took care of him and, as they grew older, he became her protector. Even today they were constantly in touch either by phone, e-mail, and sometimes by letter. Chris knew from her college days how much she loved his letters, and he kept the tradition going. She smiled again, thinking of Chris and his thoughtfulness.

Jimmy was leaning against his pickup truck when she pulled into the driveway. Jim Bradley was only an inch taller than Traci, but he looked much bigger. Built like a weight lifter, he wore khaki slacks and a golf shirt that strained at his biceps. With black hair and a dark Arizona tan, his teeth gleamed white as he grinned at Traci.

"Hi honey, sorry I'm late," she said, as she pulled up beside him.

"What! This is good for you. You're only twenty minutes late," he joked.

"Cute!" she said, throwing him the keys. "You drive, wise guy, I need the rest."

"Yes, ma'am."

A few minutes later, the Lexus pulled into traffic for the short trip to Tucson International Airport to meet the family plane.

Chapter 19

Carrie soaked until the water turned lukewarm and then reluctantly stepped out to dry off. Wearing only a terrycloth robe, she let her hair air dry while she heated up a bowl of her famous cock & bull stew. She felt relaxed as she ate and cleaned up in the kitchen. Later, sitting on the front porch, the ever present loneliness began to creep in. She decided to take a ride to Culverton Ridge.

The barn at the *Circle R* consisted of twenty stalls with a dirt floor and a hayloft above. A door on the right led to a large tack room where saddles, harnesses, and assorted other equipment hung throughout the room. Most of the stalls were empty, but Spider was waiting. He seemed to know this was a night she would need him. He whinnied when she opened the barn door, and his eyes were bright as she approached.

"Hey, Spider, you want to go for a ride tonight?" she asked, as she stroked his nose.

Spider was a black and white six year old quarter horse whose name derived from the web-like lines of black that traced across his otherwise white face. Quarter horses are powerful animals with great speed and maneuverability in tight places. They are bred for the western life and are the animal of choice for most cowboys and ranch hands.

Carrie fed him the carrot from her pocket and brushed his mane a few times. All the while, he was nudging her.

"Okay! Okay! I get the message," she said, as she threw the blanket on his back and reached for the saddle. "You're ready to go."

They left the barn at 5:00 P.M. and stopped at the bunk house to let the Wright twins know where they were going. Sudden trips to the ridge were normal for Carrie, but not an everyday event, and she wanted people to know where she would be.

Carrie had changed into jeans and riding chaps, a blue denim shirt, and a leather vest. She wore her favorite black Stetson with a red kerchief tied around her neck.

She packed her cell phone, long johns and some granola bars, a powerful flashlight, and matches in her saddlebags. She had a full canteen of water, her bedroll, and her Winchester. She didn't plan to spend the night, but it wasn't out of the question. The view from the ridge had a way of mesmerizing her, and sometimes she found it very hard to leave. If she stayed, she would call in first. The Winchester was as important as the canteen and bedroll. There were still some animals she could run into up there that she would need protection from, and Carrie was a crack shot. That came from a lot of practice and, in the beginning, a lot of patience from her husband.

Sunset would come around 7:00 P.M., and she figured they could reach the summit by 6:30. She loved the scenery on the ride up and would take her time getting there. If they returned tonight, the ride back would be slow. She would use the lantern on the way down the mountain, even though Spider had done it a hundred times and could probably make it back blindfolded.

Besides, she thought, there is supposed to be a full moon and clear sky tonight.

She pulled her headphones on as she reached the front gate. Her favorite Boccelli CD sounded in her head as she pushed Spider to a trot toward the hills to the west.

Chapter 20

Tucson International Airport always bustled with activity at this time, and today was no different. The traffic was heavy and they arrived late, at 5:20 P.M. By the time Jim and Traci found a spot in the short term parking lot, they had wasted another twenty minutes.

As they raced through the airport toward gate sixty-four, Traci glanced at her watch.

"5:30, damn! We're late," she yelled.

She didn't want her parents to be waiting for them. Her dad always wound up taxing to the same gate when he used the private plane to visit, and it was at the very end of the terminal. When they entered the gate area, Traci breathed a sigh of relief. No plane was visible on the ground through the huge windows.

"Good, they're not here yet," she gasped, trying to catch her breath.

"I'll check at the counter and see how far out they are," Jim said.

"Okay. I'm going to the ladies' room. Be right back."

A few minutes later, as Traci walked toward the gate, she wondered why Jim was still at the desk. How long could it take to get flight information? As she got closer, she noticed that Jim was agitated, talking softly but emphatically. The only words she caught as she approached sent a chill through her.

"...must have heard something from them?"

"Jimmy, what's going on?" she asked.

"I'm sure it's nothing, honey. They must have been delayed in New York because they haven't heard from them here yet," Jim answered calmly, but the look on his face belied the assurance in his voice.

"It's quarter to six, Jim. Mom would have called if they were delayed. Have they checked with Kennedy?" There was a touch of panic in her voice. Her stomach felt queasy. She didn't really know why she felt the way she did. Flights were delayed all the time. Still, she was uneasy. She was sure her mother would have called.

Jim tried to reassure her. "I've asked them to check already. There could be any number of reasons why they're late, Traci."

"Mr. Bradley…" The airline attendant who had been talking to Jim when Traci approached interrupted.

"Sir, flight 2113, a private jet from SKIPCAL CORPORATION, left Kennedy International Airport on schedule at 3:30 P.M., Eastern Standard Time, scheduled to arrive in Tucson at 5:30 P.M., Pacific Standard Time. They may have been delayed by bad weather or something else. It's still very early, and they are only fifteen minutes late. This happens from time to time. If you could take a seat, we will be right with you. We are also endeavoring to contact other surrounding airports in case they needed to land somewhere else.

"You said they were only fifteen minutes late. Why would they need to land somewhere else?" Traci asked anxiously.

"Ma'am, I'm sorry. I really don't have any answers yet. One of our airport managers is coming down to talk to you while we sort this out. If you could just take a seat, I'm sure he will be with you in a moment." The young woman behind the desk spoke calmly as she had been taught to do, but her eyes betrayed her. This was not a normal occurrence, Jim thought, as he put his arm around Traci's shoulder.

"Traci, lets sit down and let them do their jobs. There must be a simple explanation."

As they sat, she could not think of a simple explanation. Why were they asking at other airports, and why did an airport manager need to be summoned? Traci reached in her bag for a tissue and came out with her wedding checklist. Tears formed in the corner of her eyes as she sat and stared at the list in her hand.

Chapter 21

The Southwest Airlines flight from Long Island arrived at gate forty-two five minutes early. It had been a great flight. Ben slept for an hour but woke up when the stewardess came by with drinks and a snack. Skip and Ben talked for quite awhile about a variety of things, from that afternoon's game, to the wedding, to the weekend's golf matches. They had a great relationship, but didn't get to sit and talk very often.

On arrival, the plan was to catch a taxi and go directly to the rehearsal dinner at Carmine's. Skip had the directions, and the hope was that the cabby would be able to follow them, if he didn't already know of the place. Linda and the girls would meet them at the restaurant.

The line of people leaving the plane moved quicker than usual. Within a few minutes, they entered the gate area with Ben just in front of Skip. Skip almost ran into his son when Ben stopped suddenly and said, "Mom, Kerry, what are you doing here?"

In the twenty years that Skip had known his wife, the times were few when she did not greet him with a smile. This was one of those times. Something was wrong, and he knew it instantly. He glanced at his daughter. Kerry's eyes were red. It was evident that she had been crying. His eyes went back to his wife.

"What's wrong Linda? Why aren't you guys at the dinner?" he asked.

Linda hugged him and didn't let go. "Cal and Jan's plane is over an hour late."

Skip felt all the elation of the trip and the anticipation of the weekend sucked out of him. Ben just stared at Kerry in disbelief.

"How can that be?" he asked.

"I don't know. They haven't told us much," she replied in a whisper.

"What have they said, Linda? They must have told Traci something, and where is she?" Skip asked, as he made his mind focus.

"Let's go," she said, as she took his arm. "They have her upstairs in an office. Jim and his family are with her. What we know is that they left New York on time, but they haven't told us much since." She glanced at her husband as they walked. "Skip, they told us ten minutes ago that the press are starting to ask questions. I guess they caught wind of it when Jim started canceling plans for the rehearsal."

An airport official met them at a door leading to a private elevator. "Mr. Amanski, if there is anything we can do to make you feel more comfortable, please let us know."

Skip was dying inside. He would never be able to put into words what Cal and his family meant to him, but he knew he had to put those feelings aside. He reverted to a take-charge attitude that served him well in the business world.

"Thank you. First, I need to see Miss Mitchell, then your boss— or whoever is in charge. Secondly, I must insist that no one speaks to or is bothered by the press about this situation without my say so."

"That won't be a problem, sir. Let me take you to Miss Mitchell. Right this way."

The official turned and led them to an elevator. The doors opened on the third floor, and they followed the man down a corridor to a large set of offices. The words, *Tucson International Airport* and *Airport Manager, Thomas Anderson* were stenciled on the outer door. Inside, they passed through a small waiting room into a much larger office.

The Bradley's were there, along with two men and a woman that Skip did not recognize. Traci sat on the couch between Michelle and Jim. The pain on her face was like a physical blow when she looked up at him. She jumped up and threw her arms around his neck.

"Uncle Skip, I'm so glad you're here," she sobbed.

"Don't worry, honey, we'll find them," he said, trying to reassure her.

After hugs and some grim greetings, Skip turned to the other people in the room. "My name is Skip Amanski. It is my plane, my partner and, most importantly, my best friend and his family who are missing. I'm sorry if I seem brusque, but I need to know all that you know and what is being done now."

A man and a woman stood to the right of a large desk located in front of the bay window. She was the airport liaison officer, and he was the airport vice president. They both turned to the man behind the desk.

Thomas Anderson looked from person to person. His eyes flickered on Traci's face for a moment, but stopped when they met Skip's. He leaned forward and sighed.

"I'm sorry, Mr. Amanski and Miss Mitchell, but we have no answers at this time. We know flight 2113 left New York at 3:30 Eastern Standard Time. As of this moment, there has been no further contact with that flight. We have been in touch with Kennedy and with all surrounding public and private airports. No one has heard from them."

Chapter 22

Donna sat in the cockpit and watched as Bo started the 737 on a slow descent toward a private airstrip in Las Cruces, New Mexico. In the living room section, Larry Webster sat at the table playing six hands of blackjack against himself while Caitlin Sullivan sat and stared out the window. She had not moved in over an hour, and she wasn't aware that her brother has been watching her for almost as long. She worked hard to clean up her life but, after the events of the day, she wasn't sure she would ever get back to her new life on Long Island.

Sully was seething. From the time they locked the prisoners in the storage hold, he had been trying to figure out how this day had gone so wrong. They should have been cruising along the highway in a van. Instead, they were in an airplane with four hostages. For all intents and purposes, he had already killed one man. Now he would have to get rid of the plane and the other four. He didn't care about their lives, but someone would probably find the man he shot sooner or later. That put a damper on his plans for the plane and their escape. Now if they were caught, they would be looking at a murder rap instead of a drug deal. All because someone set them up. Who was it? Apart from Gomez, only his people knew the plans. Gomez didn't know the details on the New York end. It wasn't him. Bo, Larry, Donna, and Jimmy had all jumped at the idea, but not Caitlin. She fought him at first and went along only when he forced her. At the airport, she had been jumpy. At the escalator, she said he was paranoid. Before the shootings, he had to yell at her twice to get her to respond. Now, she was just plain scared. He could see it in her eyes every time anyone spoke to her.

Sully stared at the back of his sister's head. She ratted me out, he thought. She called the cops. My own sister!

He glanced around the room. It had been quiet since the trouble out back. Now, before they landed, it was time to let everyone know where they stood.

"Caitlin, I need some help out back before we land. Larry, wait here, we'll be right back. According to Bo, we should be on the ground in no time."

He tried to sound as cheerful as possible and was smiling when she turned to look at him.

"Come on, sis, in an hour we'll have all the money we ever dreamed of. No more slum living or people treating us like crap."

Caitlin got slowly to her feet and followed him. Maybe she would get away with it. Maybe he would never question what happened at the airport. One hour, and I will be free of him forever, she thought, as they walked down the aisle in the center section of the plane.

Sully stopped and turned to her. She looked up into eyes that no longer smiled. Fear scorched through her. He knew the truth.

"Please, Sully, I begged you to leave me alone. I didn't want to come. I had to do something," she pleaded.

Her breath left instantly, and she could not scream as his hands went vise-like around her neck. "You thought you could squeal on me? After I dragged you along with me your entire miserable life? Well, that won't be a problem anymore. You just made your last mistake, you ungrateful bitch," he hissed.

She kicked and tried to scream, but no sound escaped. Her brother was a strong man, and his hands felt like steel as she tried desperately to pry them apart. At first her hands clawed at his, but then, as she began to weaken, they fell by her sides. The life ran out of her, and Caitlin Sullivan died as she lived—scared, miserable, and abused.

Sully dragged his sister's lifeless body into the cargo hold and dropped her on the floor. The hostages looked up as he entered. They were bound, gagged, and freezing. He decided not to prolong the inevitable. With Kann and Caitlin dead, he would have to take one of the prisoners with him when they landed. When the authorities found the plane, they would need to find only five bodies on board. He watched them for a moment and settled on Jan Mitchell. He pulled the Magnum from the waistband of his pants. He walked to her and struck her on the temple, instantly knocking her unconscious. The two bound men strained at their ropes. Sully grinned.

"Save it boys. I'll be right back," he said, as he dragged Jan from the room.

Twenty minutes later, Sully stepped into the living room area. There would be no more trouble from anyone in the cargo hold. They would be found with the plane. He would dispose of Jan after the exchange in New Mexico. Webster met him at the door as he entered.

"Sully, I was coming to get you. Bo says we are on final approach and we should strap in."

Chapter 23

Carrie put both hands on the pommel and leaned forward in the saddle. The view from the top of Culverton Ridge was spectacular—and one she never tired of. Back over her shoulder, she saw rolling prairie dotted with outcroppings of rock, cactus, and the occasional tree. The land went as far as she could see until it seemed to merge with the sky. The trail they just traveled went back toward two distant hills where it looked more like a ribbon as it disappeared between them. Beyond the hills, the trail led to the *Circle R Ranch.*

The landscape beyond the ridge in front of her was much different. It was rougher terrain covered with thick clumps of bushes, branches, and no defined trails. The land consisted of hills and valleys of various heights, stretching out to the distant mountain range beyond which the sun would soon set in a blaze of color.

Carrie glanced at her watch. She had a half-hour until sunset, and there were things she needed to do before dark. Rory always told her, "Take care of your horse first because he is your ride home." She led Spider to a lone tree standing in the southeast corner of the clearing. After tying the reins to a branch, she poured a third of the water from her canteen into a leather feedbag. After hooking the bag to Spider's harness, she placed her bedroll on the ground along with a flashlight and a pair of binoculars.

Carrie shivered as she stood. It had grown much colder than she expected. It had reached as high as seventy degrees on the ranch that afternoon, but fall temperatures in Texas were known to drop as much as forty degrees by night's end.

If she stayed, she would have to dig out the long johns and sleep below the boulder instead of on top. The boulder was on the opposite end of the clearing, and it was massive. The chore was getting up there, but the view was worth the climb. The rock could probably hold ten men standing or five lying down, but that was only a guess.

She finished up by pouring half of the contents of a burlap bag into the feed bag. After replacing the bag on Spider, she stroked his nose.

"That should hold you for a while buddy. I'll be back soon."

With the bedroll slung across her back and the binoculars around her neck, Carrie made it to the top of the boulder fairly easily. Once there, she stood and took it all in. This was the best place to be at sunset, she told herself for the hundredth time.

From here she could see for miles in every direction. Each evening it seemed as though every color in the universe tried to squeeze underneath, as an unseen power lowered a massive curtain on another day. The light had already started to fade as the sun touched the peaks in the distance.

As Carrie bent down to unroll her bedroll, something below and to her right caught her eye. Something was out of place, something that didn't belong. She shaded her eyes and squinted. It was white, maybe a hundred yards away, like a sheet billowing each time the wind came up. She squinted harder and then remembered the binoculars hanging from her neck.

"Damn! Why not just jump up and bite me?" she said.

As she adjusted the glasses, she realized it was bigger than a sheet. Carrie couldn't figure it out at first, but slowly it dawned on her that she was looking at a parachute. She lowered the binoculars as a wave of adrenaline washed over her. Instinctively, she looked up, expecting to see a plane suspended in mid-air.

"If you can't hear a plane your probably not going to see one, you dope!" she muttered to herself. Think! If someone was on the end of that chute, is he or she still there? Are they hurt? Did they try to walk out, or was there ever a person out there at all?

Carrie made up her mind. She would have to go down there. If someone were hurt, they would probably die before anyone else found them. If they tried to walk out, she could at least track the direction they took.

It took her a half-hour to reach the chute. The terrain on that side of the ridge was nearly impassable on horseback, and the going had been very tough. She made the trip on foot, picking her way with a flashlight as day turned to night. Carrie brought her canteen, blanket, and saddlebags stuffed with whatever she might need if she found someone injured. She also carried her rifle for protection and loaded a shell in the chamber as she approached. She stopped a few yards from the white silk, not sure what to do next. Finally, she pushed aside the billowing material and found Cal lying on his right side. He looked odd, wearing only gym shorts and a ski jacket, with his skin turning a shade of blue. What she could see of the left side of his face was bruised and distorted and covered with dry—almost black—blood. She was sure he was dead and quickly knelt to feel for a pulse.

No. Maybe? Very faint if at all, she thought. She checked again at the neck. "Yes!" she said, as she felt an irregular, faint heartbeat. She bent toward his face for signs of breathing. Again, it was there, but barely. She stood, pulling her cell phone from her pocket, and dialed the ranch.

"Ryan. This is Carrie...I'm fine, but...Ryan! Shut up and listen! I found a man out here, and he is in rough shape...I don't know who he is! He was wearing a parachute, so he must have come from a plane at some point, but we don't have time for this!" Carrie yelled. She was breathing hard and exasperated by the ranch hand's questions.

"Call 911. Get a Medivac helicopter out here now! If you don't hurry, he will be dead before you get here. We are a hundred yards below the clearing on the west side of the Culverton Ridge. You know the spot. Ryan, have them land on the top if they can. If not, have them land on the other side and lead them over. No way can they land on this side. When I hear the chopper, I'll start signaling with my flashlight. Hurry, Ryan. I don't think this guy has much time left."

She pressed the *off* button and knelt back down beside Cal. She took some water to wet his lips and brushed his hair back with her hand. That's when she saw the gash on the left top corner of his forehead.

"I don't know what happened to you, fellow, but hang in there. Help is on the way," Carrie said, softly. As she panned his body with the flashlight, looking for other injuries, Carrie jumped. "Did you say something?" she asked, leaning as close to his mouth as she could. She heard him whisper in a weak, raspy voice.

"Live. Just live."

Chapter 24

At approximately 7:00 P.M., the 727 touched down on a private airfield thirty miles south of Las Cruces, New Mexico.

Bo and Donna joined the others in the center section of the plane. They had seen the welcoming committee waiting on the runway as they taxied to a stop. Now, all eyes turned to Sully.

"This day didn't go as planned," he said. "From the time we had to take this plane, everything changed. No way could we let these people go. At some point, we were going to have to deal with them. Well, I've already dealt with them and that bitch sister of mine, too." Sully paused to make sure he had their attention.

"Caitlin set us up. I'm sure of it, and she paid for crossing me. Don't make the same mistake. You're all accomplices to murder now. What happens to me happens to you. We're going to finish this deal right now. After we make the switch, we split the money and get out of here," he said.

There was silence as his words sank in. The deal had already turned into more than any of them ever bargained for.

"What happens when they find the plane?" Larry asked.

"Bo is going to dump the plane and join Donna and me in Tahoe. Worst-case scenario, they find what's left of the plane and it takes them a while to figure out whose bodies they have. Best case, they never figure it out," Sully answered.

"What about the woman?" Bo asked, pointing to Jan who they had dumped in a chair, still tied and gagged.

"She's the last loose end. She goes with us. We'll find a place to dump her. The important thing is to make this deal work," Sully said. "Get this straight. I don't trust any of them. The exchange takes place right here in this room. Larry, take a position by that door," he instructed, pointing toward the rear of the plane.

"Bo, you're at the cockpit door, so we flank them once they are on board. Donna, start unloading those bags and stack the stuff on the couch. I'll open the door and make the arrangements. Be sharp! My guess is if they get the drop on us or get the cocaine first, we won't live to see tomorrow," Sully said, as he looked around one last time.

Once everyone was in place, he turned to the door and spoke. "Time to make a deal.",Sully pulled the latch and pushed the plane door open.

Directly below the Gomez brothers waited, surrounded by four armed men that Sully didn't know. A white stretch limousine and two vans could be seen fifty yards straight out from the plane. Five more armed men stood guard by the limo. The three vehicles that Sully had requested, a Blazer, a Jeep Cherokee, and a Ford Bronco were parked to the right of the plane.

The Gomez brothers could pass for twins. Richie was 5'9", 150 pounds, where Ron was 5'8", 160 pounds. Richie, older by two years, was a nervous chain smoker who never stopped talking. Ron was more mature, calm, and quiet.

"Hey, Sully! What's up with the plane man? You got the stuff or what?" Richie yelled from the ground.

"Yeah, we've got the stuff. Where is Escalia?" Sully said.

"You know the bigwigs, Sully, they don't get involved. He's waiting in the limo until we make the deal," Richie said.

Sully looked directly at Richie Gomez.

"You tell Escalia this. It's been a bad day. Things have gone wrong from the start. People are dead, but we pulled it together, got the coke, and got it to this point." As he spoke, he let his gaze drift to the men with the guns. He wanted no surprises.

"Here's the deal, Richie. There are three and only three ways this deal can go down, and stepping off this plane to do it is not one of them," he said, pausing for effect. "First, we can have a shootout here. If anyone is still alive, winner takes all. Second, we can shut this door, fly away, and sell this stuff to someone else. Third, Escalia can come on board with three of his men, and we can make this deal as originally planned. No one gets hurt, and everyone gets rich. Those are the choices, Richie. We'll be waiting and watching."

Richie's eyes were as wide as they had ever been. "Sully, are you crazy? I can't tell Escalia what to do!" he yelled.

"I'll talk to Escalia," Ron Gomez said. He had not moved since the plane landed. Now he turned and walked toward the white limousine.

Fifteen minutes later the door to the stretch limo opened, and Juan Escalia appeared. He was a large man, not too tall, but thick, with a barrel chest and stomach to match. His wealth showed in his dress and manicure. His thick, black hair and mustache were neatly trimmed and shiny with mousse. Mostly, Juan Escalia exuded a sense of power.

He was born in the Mexican town of Sonora, one hundred miles south of the Arizona border. For five generations, his family lived in the poorest barrio in the region. He was determined to get out. He scraped, stole, fought, and killed to get to the point where he was involved in million dollar drug deals. He would not be poor again. Every business deal, legal or illegal, within fifty miles of Las Cruces came from under the umbrella of the Escalia operation. Escalia took care of the local police, courts, and politicians and, in turn, they watched out for his interests.

Today he was only interested in one hundred thirty kilos of cocaine that could upgrade the most profitable part of his empire. Escalia, in his own strange world, was a man of his word. He was a little miffed that these people would question his trust. He was not used to being questioned on anything but, for that much cocaine, he would give them the benefit of the doubt.

God be with them if they cross me, he thought, as his entourage started toward the plane.

Chapter 25

Jan Mitchell moaned and moved a bit in the chair where she had been dumped forty-five minutes earlier.

Slowly her mind came around. Images formed but made no sense. She saw Cal but couldn't reach him. He seemed to be flying. Why would he wear a ski jacket with shorts? She tried to call him but suddenly realized she couldn't talk. Everything was foggy. Her head hurt, and when she tried to touch it, her arms would not work. Then Cal was gone, and she heard voices. Her eyes snapped open. The day's events slammed into her mind with numbing speed.

The hangar! Those people! The guns! Cal killed one of them and … Oh God! They shot Cal! The blood. Cal falling. Could he be alive? If he is, did someone find him? Where are Chris and Amy? Are they okay?

Her head throbbed and she felt nauseous. She was lying in an easy chair with her feet hanging over the side. She realized that her hands were tied behind her,and her mouth was taped shut. She scanned the room, trying to focus her eyes. The tall man stood by the curtain leading to the next room. He held a gun pointed toward the plane's entrance. The blonde was on her knees, stacking something on the couch, something that looked like bags of sugar.

Jan closed her eyes tightly. She knew in order to have any chance to save her family, she would have to pay attention and get her wits back together.

She opened her eyes and looked up as the man who shot her husband entered the room.

Chapter 26

Sully stepped into the room followed by Escalia and two of his men. Escalia was out of breath. He was not used to physical exertion, and climbing the ladder to enter the plane definitely fell under that heading for him. Two things drew his attention as he took a moment to regain his wind. First, the couch where Donna stacked what would turn out to be thirty bundles of pure cocaine. Second was the woman, tied and gagged, half-sitting, half lying in an easy chair.

He surveyed the rest of the room. The woman sitting by the bags on the couch did not have a weapon that he could see. A tall man at the far end of the room stood guarding the only other entrance to the room. He counted three men with guns so far. No one would win a shoot-out here, and if they had his merchandise, he saw no need for trouble.

"Mister Sully, I am very disappointed that you would not trust me. I am a man of my word, and I do not like to talk with the guns drawn," Escalia said, while gesturing around the room.

"Look, I don't know you from Adam, but after what we went through to get here, I wasn't about to take any chances. Now that we've met, if you want to put the guns away, that's fine with me," Sully replied.

"Excellent! Muchachos, put the guns away. We will talk with our new friends. Why the plane, Senor? We were expecting vans. It was not easy to get cars and money on such short notice," Escalia said.

"The cops were tipped off in New York but, before they could spot us, we jumped this plane. They got no idea how we got away," Sully said.

"But won't they search for the plane?" Escalia asked with a worried look.

"When they find the plane, they won't find much. By the time they're done sifting through what's left of it and identifying bodies, we will be long gone. Besides, there is no way to connect you to the plane," Sully explained.

As Sully spoke, a muffled cry came from Jan Mitchell. His intentions became clear to her. She knew when he shot Cal that they would have to escape or die. Now she knew how he intended to kill them. Escalia heard the noise and motioned to Jan.

"Who is this woman?" he asked.

"She came with the plane, but we are taking her with us. There were five people on board when we took the plane, and we need the cops to find five when they find the wreck. She makes six. Things have happened today that you don't need to or want to know," Sully said.

Escalia turned to look at Jan who was now openly sobbing. He walked full circle around the chair and stopped in front of her. Jan cringed as he reached out and wiped a tear from her face.

"I am intrigued. We will speak of her later, no?" he said.

"Sure, but lets get down to business now. I assume you have the money?" Sully said.

"I do. Miguel, bring the money inside." Escalia spoke to the man closest to the outside door. Five minutes later, the man returned with two large suitcases which he placed on the table and opened. Stacked inside, row after row of unmarked bills in denominations of one to hundred dollars could be seen. Escalia pulled a silver handled switchblade from his pocket and opened it in one swift motion. He handed it to Miguel.

"Check the merchandise," he said.

"Mr. Sully, you will want to count the money, of course. Let's have a drink while the others do this job for us." Escalia grinned.

As Donna mixed drinks and the others went about the business of testing and counting, Escalia's attention turned to Jan. He liked what he saw, and he was used to getting what he wanted.

Chapter 27

The windows in the manager's office at the Tucson International Airport overlooked the runways. As Skip stood staring out at planes coming and going, he tried to think of something else to do.

Airport manager Tom Anderson offered the use of his private quarters to the families, and they accepted. He assigned one of his assistants to escort Linda, Traci, and their families to the rooms. They left minutes earlier, giving Skip time to reflect on the last forty-five minutes.

The information gathered was frustrating because there were no real answers. Airport officials in New York reported that flight 2113 had been tracked on radar from Kennedy until it was out of range. There had been no contact from the pilot after takeoff, and the plane never appeared on Tucson radar. Lastly, all surrounding airports had checked in and reported no sightings.

Skip wasted little time in assessing the situation. The people involved were competent and working diligently to find some answers, but it wasn't enough. There was only one man that he knew who could instantly take the search national.

He picked up the phone and called a number he hadn't called in twenty years. He had not spoken to Richard Ireland since he left the service. At the time, his boss told them that if they ever needed him, they knew where to find him. Employees did not become friends with Ireland, but they had done a job for him and done it well. He would always be loyal to them. His call went through immediately, and they talked briefly.

Ten minutes later, Ireland called back to say the Air Force had joined the search. They dispatched two F-16's, along with four Black Hawk helicopters to join the search, and the Arizona National Guard was told to stand by in case a ground operation became necessary. He also informed Skip that the press was reporting SKIPCAL's plane as missing, and the television stations were interrupting regularly scheduled broadcasts to report the story. Ireland promised to do what he could about the media and hung up, telling Skip to stay in touch.

71

Great, Skip thought, as he turned from the window. Just what we need. The press would hound everyone involved. Billionaires didn't disappear every day. Skip folded his arms and looked down at his shoes. It was now 7:30 in the evening and, as each minute passed, his hope for his friend's safety faded.

Chapter 28

In almost every hospital emergency room in the United States, the perception of the patients and families varies greatly from that of the on-duty staff. People who come to an emergency room come with the belief that they will be rushed into a room with a doctor and be taken care of immediately. The staff works in a matter-of-fact manner, taking each patient from check-in and the endless paper work to an examination room where a nurse takes vital signs. Within a few minutes, even if it seems like an eternity, a doctor appears; usually takes the same vital signs, assesses the situation, and treats whatever the ailment might be. The families of these patients pace the waiting room or hallways wondering if anyone in the hospital cares at all. The only time the emergency room personnel change their routine is when a life threatening case comes through the double doors.

Tonight, Carrie brought such a case to Memorial Hospital. Now, as she waited to hear the fate of the man she found, she closed her eyes and thought back on the night's events.

Forty-five minutes after finding the injured man below Culverton Ridge, Carrie heard the whine of the Medivac helicopter blades. It seemed to her that she had been sitting next to the injured man for hours. She checked his vital signs twice, but she was not sure he was still alive.

Because of the terrain on that side of the ridge, it took the paramedics, along with two *Circle R Ranch* hands, Ryan and Dave Wright, ten minutes to arrive at the bottom of the ridge. The first paramedic to reach Cal immediately started taking his vital signs. At the same time, he asked Carrie some general questions.

"Ma'am, do you know his name and have you moved him?"

"No. That's how I found him, and he didn't say his name," Carrie replied, as she backed away to give them room to work.

"Did he move at all or say anything?" the paramedic asked, as he opened the man's jacket.

"He hasn't moved, but he did speak," Carrie said. "At first I wasn't sure if it was a moan or what. Then I leaned close and could barely hear him, but I'm sure he said, "Live, just live.""

The man working on Cal looked up at Carrie as he pulled the jacket open. "Really. That's all he said? I wonder what that means?" he asked rhetorically as he turned back to his patient.

"Wow! We've got blood here," his partner said, as the bloody towels packed inside the jacket came into view under the light of Carrie's lantern. The first paramedic carefully removed the towels and reassessed the situation.

'Okay, Mike. We're going to need an IV of saline started now. This guy has been shot, and we need to repack this wound. He's lost a ton of blood," the first paramedic said to his partner.

From there things moved very quickly. One guy put in the IV while the other repacked the wound. They cut the parachute off and had the man wrapped in a blanket and strapped to the stretcher in less than two minutes.

With the help of Ryan and his brother Dave, the paramedics managed to get the stretcher back up the ridge and onto the chopper. Ryan offered to bring Spider back to the ranch, and Carrie took him up on his offer. She wanted to know what happened to the man she found.

Once they were in the air, Carrie watched the flurry of activity around the injured man in amazement as the two professionals fought to save the life of someone they had never met. She got the distinct impression that if he died, it would be a personal loss to these two men.

"Med. 25 to Memorial. Over. Med. 25 to Memorial. Come in," the man called Mike said into the hand-held transmitter.

"This is Memorial, Mike. What have you got?" an unidentified voice replied over a loud speaker.

"Male Caucasian. Between forty and fifty years old. Good physical condition. Gun shot to upper right chest. Exit wound upper right back. I think we've stopped the bleeding, but he has lost a lot of blood. There is also a head wound to the left side of his forehead that I thought was from a blow to the head or hitting a rock out here when he fell. After cleaning it, I think it may be another gunshot. Not sure on that one. We've got an IV started. Vitals: pulse very weak at around forty, but it's so faint it's hard to tell, blood pressure eighty over sixty and falling. Our ETA is twenty. We'll try to keep him alive 'til then but, like I said, he's lost a lot of blood. This is Med. 25, over."

"We'll be ready Med. 25, over and out," the voice from memorial Hospital replied.

In less than twenty minutes, they landed on top of Memorial Hospital where an emergency team was waiting. Carrie watched with renewed appreciation for the skill of these people as they transferred the injured man to a gurney and whisked him away to a waiting trauma unit. As they raced away, a nurse stepped over to Carrie.

"Let me show you to our waiting room, ma'am. It could be a while before we know anything."

Carrie turned to the paramedics who were about to board the helicopter.

"Will he live?" she asked.

"That's a tough call, ma'am. I am only guessing, but I think his loss of blood is his biggest problem. There is no way to tell until the trauma guys get a look at him, but these guys are good here," the first paramedic replied.

"Thanks. You guys were great."

"No thanks necessary, ma'am," Mike said. "That's what we do."

She shook hands with both men and followed the nurse inside to the waiting room as the chopper lifted off the roof. Time was such a strange thing, she thought. It had been a little more than an hour and a half since she found the injured man, but it seemed like days. The same nurse came by once to say the man had been taken to surgery, and there was no word on his condition. Carrie was alone, and she didn't know why shestayed. When she thought about it, she realized she had been alone for a very long time.

Chapter 29

Detective Frank Martini had this same moment every night when it was time to go home. The time of night changed, but the feeling never did. Call it loneliness or emptiness, he couldn't put his finger on it. His ex-wife had the answer; she had all the answers. He was married to the job. Being a cop was his life, and he had sacrificed everything else for it. She hit him with all the clichés when she left. They met and married while he was still in the police academy. She tried to make a home for them in a nice neighborhood, but he was never home. He meant to be, but whenever there was a tough case with overtime, he found himself volunteering. He missed one too many get-togethers with friends or neighbors before she called it quits. Thankfully there were no kids involved. The last he heard, she was living in Jersey, married to an insurance guy with two kids. When he thought of her, he had to admit he was happy for her.

If pressed, he would be forced to admit that she was right. The only time he felt complete was on the job. Home was just a place to get some fast food, a beer,and a couple of hours sleep. Tonight would be one of the tough ones, he thought. He had already punched out and was sitting at his desk with his coat on reviewing the day's events.

They had identified the entire group at the airport but had not located any of them. They had staked out all known hangouts of Mike Sullivan and Robert Boston with no results. He sent people out to Long Island where Caitlin Sullivan now lived. She had not returned home or shown up at work. They found the home and work addresses of both Larry Webster and Billy Kann but came up empty. Drug enforcement pulled in all of their informants, but no one had heard of any big drug deal going down.

He looked at his watch. It was 10:00 P.M., and his shift had ended two hours ago. Martini sighed and got up to leave. Everyone else in the squad room was watching TV; the networks were covering the disappearance of some billionaire's plane that was two hours overdue out west somewhere. He wondered why everyone got such perverse pleasure from watching these things on television hour after hour.

Martini stopped at the watch commander's desk on his way out. "Jocko. Call me if anything comes in on my case. Anything... anytime. Okay?"

Sgt. Jack Devlin looked up from his desk. "You know I will, Frank. Bad day, huh?"

Martini looked back as he stepped out into the night. "Bad day? Yeah, I would say that's an understatement, Jocko. Good night."

Chapter 30

Traci sat in the window seat and watched the lights flicker on the runway. She arrived at the airport full of excitement, which quickly turned to confusion and then fear. Now she held out just a glimmer of hope deep down in her soul that her family had not met with some sort of disaster. For two hours, Jim and his family, along with the Amanski's, had been with her, and she had needed them. She would probably need them again, but now she needed to be alone. She needed to see her family's faces in her mind.

She could see her dad, who was away a lot when she was young, but made up for lost time over the last few years. In her eyes, until Jim, all other men paled in comparison with her father. He loved her without question and supported whatever she attempted to do.

Chris was her kindred spirit. They talked and shared their ups and downs from as far back as she could remember. To this day, they kept in weekly contact either by phone or e-mail.

Traci always admired her mom. She grew up watching her and quickly learned that being beautiful and feminine didn't have to be a detriment to being a tough, intelligent woman. Her mom had shown her that she could love one man with all her heart and still be a strong, successful woman in her own right. Her mom was her best friend. Her memories flooded her mind and made waiting a little less painful.

Traci glanced at her watch. 8:00 P.M. The plane was now two and one half hours late. She shook her head. They would have been well into the rehearsal dinner by now. Jim would be there with family and friends, and she probably would have been as happy as any time in her life. It stunned her how drastically your emotions could change in an instant. Waiting was the worst. It reminded her of when John F. Kennedy Jr's plane was missing. At the time, all she could think of was Caroline Kennedy and what she must have been going through, hoping for the best, but fearing the worst. Traci said a silent prayer as she folded her knees to her chest and lowered her head to her knees.

Chapter 31

One hour after landing in Las Cruces, Bo had the 727 back in the air. Bo started his love of engines as a teenage grease monkey in local filling station in the Bronx. He drove anything he could get his hands on and taught himself to take an engine apart and put it back together. He graduated to flying while doing a four-year stint in the Army Air Corps as a mechanic. He so impressed his superiors with his knowledge of the aircraft that they sent him to flight school. Before leaving the service, he was utilized to courier planes from one base to another. Flying the 727 was a piece of cake for him.

The deal almost went off without a hitch. The money had been counted, and the Mexicans were happy with the quality of the cocaine. The vehicles Sully requested were there and ready to be loaded. The problem came from Escalia. He had no part in counting money or testing drugs. Instead, he sat on the couch, had a couple of martinis and made small talk. From time to time, he asked questions about Jan. When it came time to leave, he stood, shook hands with Sully and said, "Mister Sully, this woman is of no use to you. She will only slow you down. Why not leave her here with me?"

Sully's first thought was that it would save time and trouble not to have to dispose of her, but he didn't like loose ends.

"Sorry, pal. She can finger all of us, and I'm not leaving anything to chance."

"This is true, of course. But she can also, as you say, finger me— and I never take chances. She will never leave my hacienda alive, my friend," Escalia said.

Sully knew that she was the only person who could tell the authorities what had happened on the plane. He planned to drive some distance and ditch her along the way. He also knew that idea created the possibility of her escaping or being seen. Escalia assured Sully that in his world, she would never be heard from again. Finally, they agreed that Escalia would take Jan with him.

Escalia and his men left, taking the drugs and the woman with them. Jan did not go easily. She heard them discussing her as if she were livestock at an auction, trying to decide who would butcher her when the time came. She fought as best she could, and they had to tie her feet to get her down the ladder.

When the limo and vans left, the gang split the money, and everyone but Bo left the plane.

Larry Webster took off in a white Camaro heading north for Las Vegas. One hundred and fifty thousand dollars and Vegas—he could hardly wait. They agreed to go easy with the money at first, so as not to attract too much attention. He was sure he wouldn't need much to get on a roll. Larry felt lucky; it was his turn to get hot.

The Gomez brothers headed southeast along the coast to their final destination of Miami Beach. They got two hundred thousand a piece for their part and planned to have some fun along the way. They would stop in New Orleans for a while, and then on to Florida. For the first time in their lives, they had no timetable, no real plans— and that was just the way they wanted it.

Sully and Donna turned the Blazer west toward California. They had most of Bo's share with them and would wait for him in Lake Tahoe. Among the three of them, they had nine hundred thousand dollars.

As they drove, Sully could not get thoughts of the man he shot out of his mind. He was positive the woman would never be heard from again. Escalia would see to that. He also knew he could rely on Bo to get rid of the plane and get back to Tahoe in one piece. One thing he was sure of; if things went wrong, Bo would never talk. The one thing that kept eating at him was the guy from the plane. If he lived and someone found him, he could identify them.

What had started out as an easy exchange of coke for a ton of cash and a life of ease now hung on the hopes that this guy stayed lost in the desert.

*　　*　　*　　*　　*

Bo leveled the plane off at the lowest possible altitude. He headed it north from Las Cruces and then west toward Tucson. The plane was on auto-pilot and pointed directly at the mountains surrounding Tucson.

The plan for ditching the plane was hatched almost by accident. During the original flight, Sully was wondering out loud what to do with the plane after the deal went down when Donna said why not just let it crash. Sully was skeptical at first, but Bo was all for it. He had learned to parachute in the Army, and this would be an easy jump. He would meet up with them in Tahoe in a few days.

Now he stood in the cargo bay preparing to go. He had checked maps to find the best place to jump and not be seen. Yet, he needed to be close enough to civilization to walk out.

"I've got to pull the cord quick at this altitude," he thought.

He checked his backpack for food, matches, and canteen. Next, he grabbed the handle to open the cargo door. Hesitating, he tried to think if he had forgotten something.

He had taken Jan's watch and wedding ring and put them on Caitlin Sullivan's body. They found Cal's wallet in a travel bag and stuffed it in Billy Kann's back pocket. He secured the pilot in a cockpit chair. The others were strapped into passenger seats. Escalia's men provided a can of gasoline that he used to drench the bodies. The plan was for the authorities to think the five bodies were the five missing people. The gas was to make identifying them much more difficult, if not impossible.

Bo looked back into the plane. Should hit in about twenty minutes at this speed, he thought. He pulled the handle, grabbed the gas can, took a deep breath, and jumped.

****

The six hikers decided to pitch camp in a clearing halfway up to Timber Gorge. They were just finishing stowing their gear when they first heard the plane. It was faint at first, but grew louder by the second. It wasn't until it was almost on them that they realized the plane would hit the mountain. They instinctively dove for cover even though the plane hit five hundred yards above them. Later, they would all find different ways to describe the sound as the loudest, most terrifying thing they had ever heard. The first hiker able to gather his thoughts grabbed his cell phone and dialed 911.

Chapter 32

Thomas Anderson was a large man, nearly bald, with patches of hair on the sides and back of his head. He had been a pretty good athlete as a young man, but had a fair sized spare tire around his waist these days. He had turned sixty months earlier and he wanted to get to sixty-two to collect full social security and Medicare. It didn't seem worth it tonight.

He had been in the management end of the aviation business for thirty years, and he knew that situations like this hardly ever turned out good. He was on his third cup of coffee in the last hour. It would be a long night no matter what happened, and all search organizations were reporting directly to him.

He watched Amanski who had been standing by the big picture window for close to forty-five minutes. Skip only moved when the phone rang and only spoke to ask questions about the search. As a businessman, Anderson was a very good judge of people. The man on the other side of the room was very successful, capable, and strong; yet tonight there was no hiding his pain.

He picked up the phone by his right elbow on the first ring.

"Anderson," he said. Skip stepped away from the window and saw Anderson's head drop and his shoulder slump.

"Where?" the man said, as he started writing on a pad in front of him.

"That's about seventy-five miles east of here, right? Do you know any details? Has anyone been up there yet?" he asked. "Okay, we'll be sending a team up. I'm sure the FAA will have their guys here as soon as possible. Thanks. I'll be in touch." Anderson stood as he hung up the phone.

"I'm sorry, Mr. Amanski, but there has been a crash. The details are sketchy so far. The incident took place in the mountains seventy-five miles east of here. We believe the plane may belong to your friends."

Skip knew by the airport manager's body language that it was bad news. The pain he felt in his head was staggering. He felt as if he couldn't breathe, yet he managed to ask, "Are there any survivors?"

Anderson hesitated for a moment on how much to say but saw no reason to prolong the inevitable. "I don't have that answer, Mr. Amanski, but chances are it's not good. The call came from hikers on the mountain who said the plane slammed into the side of the mountain and burst into a ball of flame. Rescue workers are on the scene but can't get near the wreck because of the flames. We should know more very shortly." Anderson paused awkwardly. "I want you to know how sorry I am. Please sit down, Mr. Amanski. I'll get you some water and then go tell the others."

Skip straightened up and shook his head. "No. Thank you for everything, Mr. Anderson, but I'll tell them. If you could handle the press, that would be great. Just tell them the family has no comment at this time."

They shook hands, and Skip headed for the private elevator that would take him to the worst moment of his life. It would be hard enough to tell his own family, but it was facing Traci that he really dreaded. The elevator doors opened into the foyer of Thomas Anderson's private apartment. The door to the main suite was directly in front of him. Two smaller suites were to his right and left. He knew Traci was in the master suite. How do you tell someone that you love like your own child that her whole family is likely dead? The truth of that thought took his breath away each time it entered his mind. He knew he had to push his own feelings away. He knocked softly and entered the room. Traci was still sitting alone in the window when Skip entered. She looked at him, and her lower lip began to tremble.

"They're gone, aren't they, Uncle Skip?"

He crossed the room to her. He wanted desperately to soften the blow for her, but he did not know how. "The plane crashed, honey. They don't think anyone made it out." She fell into his arms sobbing and, as she did, tears started to stream down his cheeks.

Chapter 33

Jan was lying face down on the floor between the seats in one of the vans. It was a short but uncomfortable ride before the van came to a stop. When the doors opened, someone cut the rope around her ankles and yanked her to her feet by the waistband of her jeans.

She found herself standing in a large courtyard surrounded by a five foot high stone wall. There was an oversized garage located along the west wall and a guesthouse on the east wall. Two guardhouses flanked the main gate behind them. Directly in front of her stood what could only be described as an adobe mansion.

The men were all speaking Spanish which she didn't understand, but it was clear to her that Escalia was giving the orders. When he stopped speaking, they started carrying the bags from the plane into the house. He then pointed to her and spoke again. Immediately, two men took hold of her arms and led her toward the front door. Inside, the house was immaculate with dark mahogany woodwork and ceilings. The floors were finished hardwood, and the décor was antique Spanish-American.

They led Jan down a series of hallways and into a massive, fully furnished bedroom. The room had a large, walk-in closet and a connecting bathroom. The furnishings included dressers on opposite walls with a large oval mirror by the main door. A padded bench sat at the foot of a four-poster bed that was the centerpiece of the room.

As soon as they entered, the two men pushed her to the middle of the room, untied her, and ripped the tape from her mouth. She yelped in pain, but they took no notice and quickly left the room.

Jan was in a daze. Her mind couldn't comprehend all that had happened in the last few hours. She made her way to the bench and sat. Why was she here? Why was she still alive? Could Cal, Chris, and Amy really be dead? Those thoughts were just starting to filter through her head when the door opened and Juan Escalia entered. She quickly jumped to her feet.

"Senora. Please stay seated. You have had a trying day."

Jan did not move or speak.

"You must be thirsty and hungry. My people will bring whatever you would like," Escalia said with a smile.

Again Jan made no reply. Escalia's eyes narrowed, and his smile disappeared. He stepped close to her and spoke in a whispered but threatening tone.

"Let me explain the situation very clearly. You would be dead if the people from the plane had taken you with them. I have prolonged your life. How long that will last depends on how long I am pleased by your presence here. You belong to me now. You should be proud that I have selected you. Make no mistake, keep my interest—and you will live."

Jan felt her skin crawl as he walked around her.

"I promise that I will enjoy myself. The only question is how hard I will need to work for my pleasure. There is no escape. There is only one way to leave here. Be smart and enjoy yourself while you can. Nothing will happen to you as long as I am happy with you. Do you understand, Senora?"

Jan stood silently staring at him.

Escalia smiled broadly and stroked her cheek. "I do not think you are so tough. I will leave you now. I must finish the day's business before I come to you. The bathroom is there for you to freshen up, and clothes have been laid out for you. In an hour's time I will come back to you, and then we shall see. Until then, adios, Senora," he said.

He turned and left, locking the door behind him. As the door closed, Jan slumped to the floor. She felt drained mentally and physically as the day's events washed over her. It seemed surreal—like a nightmare—but three things continued to pound at her heart. Chris was dead, her baby boy. She remembered her pregnancy with Chris and how much harder it had been than with Traci. She was sick most of the way, and labor had been brutal. Then, it was over and the nurse laid him on her chest in the delivery room. From that moment right up through his wedding to Amy last summer, he had been nothing but a joy to her. Now, they were both gone.

Oh, God! The wedding. Traci would be devastated. How would she get through this? "Traci. I love you," she whispered.

Finally, her thoughts turned to Cal. Could he still be alive? She cried as she thought of the last time she saw him. No, he could not have survived. Realization started to set in. In one day they had taken her son, daughter-in-law, and husband. They had taken her freedom. They had killed her life. Her feelings of self pity and despair turned to hate and resolve. Cal would fight; but how? She looked up at the door. Escalia would be back soon, and he made it clear what would happen when he did.

As Jan stood and looked for a way out, the adrenaline started to rush through her body. She ran to the bathroom almost in a panic—searching for something—anything.

Hanging from a hook by the mirror, she saw a negligee. It was beautiful, floor length, white and sheer. This was what he meant. The clothes laid out for her. She watched her reflection in the mirror for a moment. Her panic disappeared and, in those few seconds, she made a decision. She wrapped a towel around her hand and punched the mirror as hard as should could, shattering it.

Chapter 34

Jerry Yacamata was Chief of Emergency Surgery at Memorial Hospital and Medical Center. When he walked into the waiting room in the Trauma Center, he found Carrie Douglas sleeping on the couch. She seemed in an odd position to him. She looked as if she were a puppet suspended by strings, sitting on one foot with her hands at her sides and her head lolling to the right. He hesitated for a moment. She probably needed her sleep, but so did he, and he couldn't hit the doctors' lounge until he talked to her.

"Ma'am," he said, as he tapped her shoulder. Carrie awoke with a start. "I'm sorry, ma'am. I didn't mean to startle you."

She studied the slightly built man who stood over her. He wore green hospital scrubs with a stethoscope hanging from his neck. Yacamata was a second generation Japanese American with strong Asian features and piercing black eyes.

"I'm Doctor Yacamata. I operated on your husband," he said.

"He's not my husband. In fact, I don't even know him. Is he going to be okay?" Carrie asked.

"Do you know how we can get in touch with his family?" Yacamata asked.

"No. Like I said, I don't know him. I found him injured out by Culverton Ridge and called 911. I would really like to know if he's going to be all right," she explained.

"He is in intensive care right now. He lost a great deal of blood, and we had to rectify that through transfusions. As soon as his condition stabilized, we took him to the OR." Yacamata paused as if to gather his thoughts.

"We were able to repair the gunshot wounds. Actually, he was a lucky guy in two regards. The bullet in his chest went straight through without hitting any vital organs and, somehow, the shot to the head bounced off. He must have been turning when he was shot. It's rare when someone gets shot twice, once in the head, with as little physical damage as this guy has."

"Does that mean he is going to live?" Carrie asked.

"It's too early to tell. He is in very serious condition, mostly due to loss of blood. The next twenty-four hours will be critical for him. He may still need another transfusion." Again, he paused.

"I'm not sure it matters to you if you don't know the man, but we have contacted the police. It's required anytime a gunshot wound comes to Memorial. He didn't tell you his name, but did he say anything that might help to identify him?" Yacamata asked.

"He only spoke once when I first found him, but he didn't say his name. All he said was, "Live, just live," Carrie answered.

Yacamata raised his eyebrows. "Interesting. Something kept him alive out there. Maybe he just kept telling himself to live. If you hadn't found him when you did, he wasn't going to live much longer," he said.

It was at that moment that Carrie surprised herself. It was true that she knew nothing about him, but she had found him close to death. Now she wanted to see him safe, with people caring for him.

"Can I see him?" she asked.

Yacamata hesitated for a moment. Normally only families are allowed to visit patients in ICU. The family wasn't there, and she had saved the man's life—at least temporarily. He decided to make an exception.

"I don't see why not. We have him in a private room on the third floor until the police talk to him. I'll take you up myself," he said.

Chapter 35

Skip called Linda and Jim from Traci's room. When the families arrived at the master suite, the tears started all over again. They all tried to help each other deal with the crushing news. They talked and cried and remembered. After an hour, they decided to leave Jim and Traci alone. Linda made sure Jim would call her if he thought Traci needed her at any time during the night.

As he held Linda's hand and walked with his family toward their room, Skip couldn't get one thought out of his mind. Everyone in Traci's room, himself included, kept referring to Cal, Jan, and the kids in the past tense. That wasn't good enough for him. He had to know more.

"I'm going to the crash site. I have to see for myself. We have no closure. I have to know what happened to them. All we know is what we have been told. I have to go out there, Linda," he said, stopping in the middle of the foyer.

"We all need to know, especially Traci. There are no answers here," Linda said.

*   *   *   *   *

The side of the mountain below Timber Gorge resembled a huge Hollywood movie set. The searchers set up a series of portable spotlights that lit up the crash site. The parameters of the site stretched five hundred yards in every direction. The investigators agreed that the debris field was sure to widen in the morning light.

Skip stood on the outskirts of the lights surrounding the smoldering rubble. He had returned to Anderson's office and, within fifteen minutes, was boarding a helicopter with a search team heading for the crash site.

He could see officials from the FAA and the Tucson International Airport sifting through the debris with flashlights. Skip looked at his watch. 11:45 P.M. It had taken all of three hours to put out the fires, and it would be a long time before they had all the answers they were looking for.

Skip had come to this place for one reason—to find out the fate of his friends. As he looked up at the mountain, he was sure of one thing. No one on that plane had survived the crash, and he had no reason to believe his friends were not on board.

He looked again at the one section of the plane that stood intact. It was a large rectangular piece of the tail section with the name SKIPCAL stenciled across in bright red letters. He sat on a rock to watch and wait.

Chapter 36

Juan Escalia strode down the long corridor in the left wing of his mansion. The house was divided into three distinct sections. The right side held the living quarters of the Escalia family, which consisted of Juan, his wife, and seven children.

The Escalias lived what they considered to be a normal Mexican family life. Juan went to work each day and came home each night. He loved his family dearly and doted on his children to excess. The kids went to school in town. Of course, they went under armed guard, and he owned the town. Still, they thought everything was normal. His wife did what, in her mind, a dutiful wife should do. She cooked and cleaned for her family. She cared for their children. She shopped and gossiped with the local Mexican women. She never asked about her husband's business or what he did when he was away from home. She did not want to know. He loved her and took care of her and her babies; that was all that mattered.

Escalia conducted his business in the middle section of the main house. It consisted of Escalia's company offices, meeting rooms, a conference room, and assorted guest rooms.

Entertainment was the main theme to the left side of the building. There was a game room, a bowling alley, a billiard room, an indoor pool, and four lavishly furnished bedrooms. In the bedrooms, Escalia participated in his favorite hobby. He enjoyed bedding women, both willing and unwilling, the way most men enjoyed a round of golf. Sometimes things went as planned, sometimes not, but he almost always enjoyed himself. Usually the women who found themselves in one of his rooms were young and eager, young and scared, or young and desperate. Almost all of them wound up working the streets for him when he tired of them. The rest would not be heard from again.

Tonight he was extremely excited about the woman from the plane. She was very attractive and well built, he thought, as he approached the bedroom door. What fascinated him was how a mature, intelligent, rich woman would react to being helpless and forced to give in to him.

His business had taken longer than expected. Afterward he changed into silk pajamas and robe. Escalia took the silver switchblade from his bathrobe pocket and looked in the mirror by the door.

"Better she knows where she stands from the beginning, my friend," he said to his smiling image.

When Escalia unlocked the door and stepped in, he stopped dead in his tracks. He wasn't sure what he expected, but it was not this.

Jan was a beautiful woman who attracted attention wherever she went and, on those occasions when she wanted to look good, she was a knockout. She may never have looked better than she did when the bedroom door opened.

She had washed and dried her hair, and it flowed from her shoulders with a brushed, but wild, look. She wore a little more makeup than normal to accentuate her eyes and lips. She was barefoot and wearing the negligee that he had left for her. The gown was a perfect fit, and she was obviously naked under it. The outline of her hips and breasts could easily be seen through the material. She stood tall. With her shoulders back, her nipples could be seen in the outline of the material. It was not hard for her to let tears form in the corners of her eyes.

Her beauty struck him. Never had there been a woman such as this in his room.

"Senora. You surprise me. Am I to believe by your appearance that you will come willingly to me?"

Jan answered in a trembling voice, "My name is Janice. Please don't hurt me any more."

Escalia's emotions were working overtime as he turned and locked the door. He put the switchblade back in his pocket. He could not remember being this turned on. Yet, it seemed unreal. Was it possible she could just give in to him? He needed some assurance.

"Janice is a beautiful name. I could not have hoped for your cooperation, but I can promise as long as you can please me that you will not be hurt again. Will you do as I ask to please me, Janice?"

She blinked her eyes to let the tears flow and nodded her head yes.

Escalia stepped across the room and stood only a foot away. He could smell her now and see the tears and fear in her eyes. He grew even more excited, if that was possible. He moved his hands between her arms and her sides, sliding the silky material to touch her hips. He leaned forward to put his lips on her neck.

She felt the breath on her skin as she raised her right arm from the folds of the gown. Clutching the jagged piece of glass wrapped in a facecloth, she plunged it as deeply as she could into his neck. The pointed end went in a good four inches, and the blood spurted like a small geyser. She stepped back and watched as Juan Escalia died.

His head jerked up, and his hands grabbed at the glass embedded in his neck. He looked like a dog chasing his tail as he spun around, succeeding only in cutting his fingers. His eyes were wide and frantic, and the only sound he made was a prolonged gurgle.

Jan sat on the bench and watched as he sank to the floor. He may not have killed her loved ones, but he started the deal that ruined her life and then believed he could take her, too. She had never hurt any living thing in her life, but as he pleaded with his eyes for help, she leaned close and said, "Die, you bastard."

* * * * *

Jan looked at the clock on the night table. It was midnight. An hour had passed since she stabbed Escalia and he had long since stopped moving. What do I do now, she thought. The exhilaration of killing Escalia had been replaced by despair. Her family was still dead or in a place where she could not reach them. At some point, Escalia's people would find out about their boss. She was sure she would die at that point. She had seen the place when they arrived. It was a fortress with armed guards everywhere. There was no chance of escape. She knew her life would end here. The only question was how.

She looked down at the clothes she was wearing and then at the bed. She stared for a moment at the man on the floor and the massive pool of blood that had formed around him. She would not let them find her like this.

She made up her mind, stood up, and walked to the bathroom. She let the gown drop to the floor and dressed in her own clothes. She washed her face of all make-up, brushed her hair, and put it in a ponytail. She turned the light out and returned to the bedroom where she leaned over Escalia's body and took the switchblade from his pocket.

She turned out all the lights except the one on the nightstand and lay on her back on the left side of the bed. She closed her eyes, and tears rolled down her cheeks as she whispered, "Please forgive me, Traci."

Jan tried to think of the happiest moment of her life, but all she could think of was making love with Cal. It would be one of those times when she knew he was coming to her. She would be in bed under the covers, wearing only a T-shirt. There would be one dim light somewhere in the room, and she would watch the bathroom door in anticipation. He would come to her from across the room, wearing nothing. God, how she loved to look at his body. Then he would be over her, running his hand down her hip as he lifted her and entered her all at the same time. How she loved this with him.

She opened the switchblade and prepared to make deep parallel cuts in her left wrist. If she were going to die here, it would be by her own hand. She felt the sharp blade cut into her skin. As she did, Cal was there again—over her—holding her. He whispered in her ear, "Live baby! Just live!"

She dropped the knife and sat upright in the bed. Oh God, Cal, she thought. I'm so sorry. What was she thinking? She had begged Cal to stay alive. He would want her to do the same. Find a way to get to Traci as long as you are alive. You have to try, she thought. Her wrist was bleeding, but not too bad. She went to the bathroom and found a couple of Band-Aids and some gauze in the medicine cabinet and quickly bandaged her wrist.

Back in the main bedroom, she tried to figure out her options. The windows were small, rectangular, and high up on the wall. She could get to them but probably not fit through. Her only option was the door.

She unlocked the deadbolt and leaned against the door as she opened it a crack. The hallway was empty, and she held the knife tightly as she eased out. She was not going out without a fight. It was after midnight, and this portion of the house seemed deserted. She made her way in her bare feet through a labyrinth of hallways, stopping at every corner, expecting to find an armed guard at each one. She found no one until she reached the ground floor.

Through the small window by the outside door, she watched the two guards share a cigarette. She could see the guardhouses across the compound by the front gate. There were no men stationed there. She would have no sight line to her right or left until she got outside. Taking a deep breath, she opened the door and stepped out. The temperature had dropped to fifty degrees, which still seemed warm to Jan, having come from New York in October. The two men swung around to face her as the door opened.

"Hey, guys, can I bum a cigarette?" she said, with the warmest smile she could muster. Both men put a hand on a weapon as one man spoke with a heavy Spanish accent.

"Who are you? Where have you come from?"

So far, so good. They obviously had not been on the plane or they would have recognized her instantly. "I just left your boss. He's asleep. I guess he was more worn out than I thought," she laughed. "I decided to get some fresh air, and the cigarette sure looked good. You got an extra?"

The two men relaxed a little and grinned at each other. One brought out a pack of Winston Lights as the other circled around her.

"I am Carlos, and this is my friend, Enrique, Senora. I think the boss is a lucky man?" he said, with a leer.

She took the cigarette and grinned. Looking up and down both men's bodies with as much appreciation as she could manage, she said, "Maybe you could get lucky, too. I could go for a couple of young studs for a change, but there will be trouble if we get caught."

They immediately took the bait. This woman was high class. Better than any woman they could find at one of the local clubs.

"No one is awake. One at a time is okay, no? The other can stand watch," Enrique offered. Then, hesitating, he asked, "What happened to your arm, Senora?"

Jan stepped forward and ran her hands through the hair of the man who had spoken.

"Things got a little rough earlier. It's no big deal," she answered, and then added, "One at a time sounds good to me. Who's first and where? Not here in the middle of the courtyard." She laughed.

At this point, the man had his hands all over her body and was already leading her back inside as he told his partner, "Stand watch, Carlos. I will leave plenty for you. This way, Senora, there is a room just inside we use to rest in when we are on duty."

Carlos watched longingly as Enrique half dragged her by the hand back inside.

As the door to the bedroom closed behind them, Jan pulled Enrique close and grunted in pain. "Ouch! We won't be needing this," she said, as she pulled his gun from the waistband of his pants.

"Careful with that thing. You'll kill somebody." The man laughed.

Jan quickly backed away, pointing the gun at his head. "That is exactly what I will do if you make even one sound. Make no mistake. I'm desperate. Your boss is dead, and you will be too if you don't do what I say."

Enrique was seething. A woman had duped him, and she had his weapon; but the look on her face told him he had better do as she said. She kept the gun on him as she searched the room. She found socks in the dresser and ties in the closet. She threw them at her prisoner.

"Stuff the socks in your mouth and tie your feet with one of the ties. Tight, don't try to fool me," she ordered.

When he finished she told him to tie his right arm to the bottom of the bedpost with another tie. Finally, when he was nearly immobile, she finished the job by tying his left arm to his right and tying the last tie around his head to secure the gag. The whole process took fifteen minutes. She left him there and turned her attention to the second guard. As she stepped out, she quickly checked to see that on one else was in the plaza.

Carlos was wary and reached inside his jacket as she smiled and came toward him.

"Next," Jan said.

"That was quick. Where is Enrique?" he said.

"He wants you to join us," Jan said, as she put her arms around him.

He pushed her away. "He wouldn't do that. He knows someone must stay on duty. Where is he?" Carlos said. He was not smiling now. As he looked to the door leading inside, she started backing toward the outside gate. Suddenly, he lunged and grabbed her, dragging her toward the door.

"Let's go see Enrique. Something's not right."

Jan plunged the switchblade deep in his ribs. He screamed and fell to his knees, letting go of her arm as he did. She turned and ran for the gate like she had never run before. She ran for Chris and Cal and especially for Traci. She had to escape to reach Traci.

Carlos was badly wounded. The blade slid between two ribs and punctured his lung. He would need immediate medical attention, or he would drown in his own blood. Yet, somehow, he managed to roll on his side and empty his weapon at the fleeing woman. His sight was clouded and his hand was shaking, but two bullets hit their mark.

Jan had almost reached the guardhouse when she felt as if someone punched her in the back. The blow knocked her to the ground. Her eyes closed and she could not move. It felt as if her back were on fire.

Then, suddenly, Cal was holding her in his arms. She smiled. She felt safe, and the pain disappeared as the sounds of footsteps and shouts faded in her ears.

Chapter 37

The Intensive Care Unit at Memorial Hospital consists of a large ward with fifteen beds and two private rooms. Detective Sam Lowery paced back and forth in front of a uniformed police officer outside the door to one of the private rooms. He was smoking a cigarette in direct defiance of the *No Smoking* signs posted in clear view throughout the hospital. Lowery rarely paid attention to rules and regulations, and tonight was no different. He was in no mood to care what anyone thought. As usual, Chief Nicolls had given him the crap job.

Lowery had been with the Midland Police Department for two years after escaping a scandal-ridden career in Las Vegas by the skin of his teeth. He weaseled his way through allegations of kickbacks, bribes, and sexual favors from the Vegas hookers for ten years. When the woman he had been with the night before turned up missing, he was offered a chance to transfer out or be prosecuted. There was no hard evidence against him, but he knew they would love to pin any crime on him. His bosses knew he was bad and had been looking for a way to get rid of him for a long time. What they didn't know was that he was guilty. They had too much to drink, and she tried to hold out on him. When he demanded his monthly protection cut and some action, she laughed at him. He hit her hard, but it was her head hitting the sidewalk cornerstone that killed her. He made sure the body would never be found, and there were no witnesses to the murder. But he had been seen with her earlier that night and knew it was time to move on.

Chief Nicolls took on the transfer knowing full well who Lowery was, and he kept a thumb on him from the time he arrived. In Lowery's mind, waiting to see some guy who had been found wandering in the desert was just another in a long line of fluff cases Nicolls had handed him. Not once in two years had Lowery been the primary on a big case. He was usually assigned to car thefts, shoplifting, or other minor offenses. He had had enough. He was looking for a way out.

Lowery stubbed his cigarette out on the side of a trash can and threw the butt in as Dr. Yacamata and Carrie Douglas approached.

He managed to put on his most sympathetic face as he stepped forward and extended his hand to Carrie.

"Ma'am, I'm Detective Sam Lowery. Sorry to hear about your husband's injuries. Okay if I ask you some questions?"

"He is not related to me. I've already told a few people here that I don't know him. I simply found him out there injured and called for help."

"Really?" Lowery said, with an air of disbelief in his voice. "Well, I still need a statement from you. Doc, when can I talk to this guy?" he said, dismissing her for the time being.

"Mrs. Douglas has asked to see him, but as far as questioning him, that is impossible right now. Even if he had regained consciousness, which he has not, his condition is in such a weakened stated that any exertion could have a disastrous effect," Yacamata answered.

"Look, Doc, She ain't related to this guy. If she goes in, so do I," Lowery stated.

Yacamata had dealt with Lowery before and had a strong dislike for him. He was easy to dislike, and the look Carrie gave him showed the instant disdain she felt for the detective's arrogant, pushy manner.

"You gotta do what you gotta do, lady," he said, as he grinned and shrugged his shoulders.

"All right. You can both come in, but only for a short time. And no questions, Detective. Understood?"

Lowery put both hands up in a defensive manner. "No problem, Doc."

The bed was on the right side of the room as they entered. The curtain above the bed had been pulled back so that Cal was in full view. He was covered to his sternum with a sheet and blanket. Just above the blanket, his right chest was bandaged. A thin tube could be seen leading out from under the bandage somewhere to the right of the bed and out of sight. An IV drip hung from a stand on the left side of the bed and was attached to his wrist. The vital sign monitors were above the bed with various wires snaking down to the appropriate parts of Cal's body. The only other signs of injury were the bandages wrapped at an angle across his forehead and around his head. The bruising and swelling on the left side of his face was extensive, making his features distorted. It would have been tough for a family member to recognize Cal in his condition.

"How long will he be out, Doc?" Lowery asked, just a little too loud.

"Keep your voice down. There is no way that I can answer that question. I can only say that I think we have saved his life, but even that is not a certainty," Dr. Yacamata whispered. "Did you want to speak to him, Mrs. Douglas?" he asked. "I'm pretty sure he can't hear you, but I can't see how it can do any harm."

Carrie did want to reassure the man but didn't know why or what to say to him. "It's Carrie, and no, as I said, I don't even know him."

Lowery had been watching her closely and noticed her hesitate. Maybe there is something going on between these two, he thought.

"In that case, why don't we sit down and you can fill me in on how you just happened to find a guy with two bullets in him somewhere in the desert," Lowery offered sarcastically. Before she could answer, Dr. Yacamata stepped across the room and put his hand on the doorknob.

"Not in here, Detective. Take it outside," he said.

"Okay. Let's get this over with," Carrie said.

As she stepped toward the door, Lowery pulled a tiny slide camera from his pocket and snapped two quick pictures of the injured man.

Dr. Yacamata spoke almost before the second flash had faded, and he was seething. "How dare you! You have no right to take pictures in here without permission," he snapped.

"Hey, no harm done. What's the big deal?" Lowery grinned, sticking the camera back in his pocket and circling toward the door.

Carrie was not paying attention. The man in the bed had moved.

*   *   *   *   *

Cal felt as if he were swimming upstream toward something in the distance. What was it? Keep swimming, he told himself. It was something he had to reach. Voices! I hear voices, but I don't recognize them. Keep swimming! Suddenly, a blinding light hit him, and he knew he wasn't swimming. He was waking up from a deep sleep. He tried to open his eyes, but couldn't. Again, the light! Open your eyes, he told himself. This time he did, but only for a second, as the bright light above the bed hit his eyes. He heard a woman's voice.

"Hey! He's awake. Turn that light off! It's right in his eyes," Carrie yelled.

When the light went out, he opened his eyes again. There were three people in the room, two men and a woman. He did not know them.

"Where am I?" he asked in a weak voice.

"You are in the Intensive Care Unit of Memorial Hospital," a man in a white coat with a stethoscope around his neck answered. As Cal became aware of his surroundings, he could feel the bandages and wires attached to him.

"Why am I in the hospital?" What happened to me?" he asked.

"You were shot twice. This woman found you out on the prairie and called 911," the same man answered.

"Shot? Prairie? Where are we?"

"We are in a hospital in Midland, Texas, pal, and we thought you might fill us in on the shooting," the other man said in an accusing voice.

Cal grimaced. He began to become aware of the pain from his injuries.

"I'm sorry, but I don't remember being shot."

"That is not important right now. You've had a very traumatic experience. What is important is that you rest and get better. If you could let me know how to contact a relative, we could tell them you are here and that you are okay, Mr...." Dr. Yacamata tried to reassure him.

Fear started to rise from deep in Cal's stomach. Everything they said registered with him. He understood that he was hurt. He also understood that he was in a hospital. He knew about Texas and where it would be located on a map, but he could not answer the last question.

Dr. Yacamata could see the confusion on his face.

Detective Lowery saw fear and wondered if it was real or manufactured.

Carrie watched as a lone tear rolled down Cal's right cheek.

"I don't know who I am," Cal said, his voice quivering.

The only sound in the room was the beeping of the alarm on Dr. Yacamata's wristwatch, signaling midnight and the end of a long day.

Chapter 38

Cal stepped down from Carrie's front porch and headed across the compound toward the main barn. Reaching the door, he turned to see Carrie still standing on the porch where he had left her. She stood watching the trail of dust from Detective Lowery's Jeep as it disappeared in the distance. Cal watched her longingly for a moment. It seemed incredible to him that he had met her only three months earlier upon waking up in his hospital room.

Entering the barn, Cal stopped to take a deep breath. He loved the aroma of this place. The combination of horses, hay, dirt, and manure gave off a distinctive smell, and he knew all of those smells. He knew where they came from. He knew how to saddle a horse. He knew he was in Texas. In fact, he knew the history of Texas: the Alamo, Sam Houston, Davey Crockett, and Sam Bowie. He probably could recite all fifty states, but he did not know how he knew these things. He couldn't remember when or where or from whom he had learned these things. Every hour of every day he went through these same agonizing thoughts.

The working horses of the *Circle R.* ranch were all quarter horses. Cal walked from stall to stall, whispering and patting each horse that came forward. He lingered with Spider for a moment, thinking of Carrie and the long rides they had taken together over the last few months.

Last night, their ride led them to Culverton Ridge, and she had shown him the spot where she found him. He was getting better each day, but not good enough for a return trip the same day; and so they spent the night. She told him it was her favorite spot in the world and that she had never taken anyone else there. He knew he could have kissed her, and maybe more.

Carrie had made it clear over the last month how she felt about him. Every fiber of his being wanted her. She was beautiful and sensitive; she had saved his life and brought him to her home. He loved the ranch and her way of life, but would he feel the same way if he woke up tomorrow with his memory intact? That was the question that kept haunting him.

Each stall had a small wooden sign hanging over it with the horse's name burned into the wood. The sign over the stall next to Spider's read *Midnight.* Midnight's coat was shiny and black as coal. Every inch from nose to tail was black except the whites of his eyes. He came forward as Cal stopped at his stall. He was proud, and his eyes were bright. He snorted as Cal stroked his nose.

"Do you know me, black beauty? No? Well, join the crowd."

He asked that question in his head of every person he met since he woke up in the hospital. Usually he stared them down until they turned away. The doctors told him he could go home after a few weeks in the hospital. Carrie offered her ranch as a temporary place for him to stay until he could recover. The doctors warned him that even if someone came forward and recognized him, it wouldn't necessarily follow that he would get his memory back. When it was time to leave the hospital, the nurse handed him a release form to sign. The name on the form read *John Doe.*

Carrie had been unbelievable. In the beginning she cleaned his wounds, changed his bandages, and cooked for him. She saw to it that he had clothes to wear, and she sat up at night and talked until he fell asleep. Lately, he looked forward to her smell and the incidental touch of her hands. As much as he tried, he could not help being attracted to her.

He remembered all of it as he brushed Midnight's tail and mane. The motion was more therapeutic for him than Midnight. His range of motion was still limited, and there was still some stiffness whenever he used his right arm; but each day it got better, and he had been riding for six straight days now.

He decided that he could not go on like this until he got answers about who he was. It was not fair to Carrie, and he had to know for himself. He called Lowery the night before and asked him to come out to the ranch. Lowery had been dogging him almost every day, both in and out of the hospital. Cal knew that Lowery didn't trust him, and he didn't care. So what if he thought Cal was faking. If he was any good at what he did and found out who Cal was, it would all be worthwhile. He loved the ranch, and his feelings for Carrie got stronger every day; but he knew it wasn't real. Every night when he went to bed, he was sure he would wake up and know who he was. Each morning when he looked in the mirror, a stranger looked back.

Chapter 39

Carrie watched as Lowery's Jeep disappeared from sight. She sat on one leg in the porch swing and rocked herself with the other foot. Closing her eyes, she leaned her head back and sighed.

"What the hell are you doing?" she asked herself out loud.

Three months ago she was living a simple, quiet life watching the sunset from her favorite spot in the world. Now, she found herself caught up with a guy who had been shot twice and dumped out of a plane, she guessed, who didn't know his own name.

Lowery was a jerk. She hated him, and she reserved that feeling for very few people. He made it clear that he believed she was involved in some scheme with the injured man, though he came short of accusing her. She knew he had a job to do, but he was arrogant and abrasive. After he called her honey and babe the first few times, she stopped him in mid-sentence and made it clear that he was to refer to her as Mrs. Douglas and nothing else.

Though she disliked Lowery, she knew he was right about the injured man. He could very well be involved in something criminal, and he could be dangerous.

The doctors told her there was no telling how long the amnesia would last or what he would be like when he came out of it, if he ever did. Brett, her foreman, was also concerned. He warned her not to get too close to Cal.

She talked with Cal long into the night more than once. She watched him with the horses. She taught him to ride and, finally, she brought him to the ridge. He was quiet and gentle, but strong and handsome. The night before on the ridge was perfect, and she had grown comfortable with him. She wanted him to kiss her. She wanted him to make love to her, and she let him know that she was willing. Carrie curled up on the swing and shook her head. She was falling in love with him.

Chapter 40

Lowery brought the Jeep to a rolling stop at the end of the access road leading away from the ranch. He turned right onto Highway 90 and headed back toward Midland. The question was what to do when he got there. The amnesia guy had asked to see him. He wanted new pictures and fingerprints circulated in a renewed effort to determine his identity. To Lowery, a man found in the middle of the desert, shot twice and wearing a parachute, had illegal activity written all over it. As for the woman, he wasn't convinced she found him by accident. Obviously something was going on between the two of them. Lowery glanced at the folder on the seat next to him. He wanted to stay in control of the situation, but the man insisted. He would have to put the new information in the system now.

Take thing slowly, he thought, as he pushed the Jeep's speed up over the eighty mark. I gotta make sure I come out on top if there is any money to be made in this deal.

From the beginning he was convinced that the guy was hiding something, either to protect himself or someone else. The surrounding airports reported no missing planes or people. Lowery circulated the man's picture and a story about him in the local papers the day after he woke up, and no family had come forward looking for the injured man. Three months later the man still claimed to have no memory. For a few days he gave daily reports to Chief Nicolls. Then, he decided to keep the investigation as quiet as possible. He let the case be buried, filing reports at longer intervals before stopping all together.

He knew the guy disliked him, and the Douglas broad liked him even less. Who cares, he thought. She's probably involved in some scheme with the guy. Lowery had checked her out right away, and her reputation turned up spotless—both socially and in the business world.

The report meant nothing to him. Lowery trusted no one. He started out as a uniformed police officer in Las Vegas, using anyone and anything he could to move up the ladder to detective. Once there, he established himself as a very good investigator, but one who was hated by his peers. He had used them all in one way or another, and there were some happy people when he was forced to transfer or lose his shield. Life changed for him in Midland. He was no longer a big wheel. Lowery was a nobody, and he didn't like the feeling. He wanted out of the department rat race. He wanted a big score. He thought the unknown man and the cowgirl just might lead him there.

Chapter 41

Traci sat in her office and stared at the stack of sympathy cards piled on her desk. She picked up the top card and reached for her letter opener. The inscription on the gold handle caught her eye—TRACI'S KID'S. She turned it over to read the words she knew would be there: *Good Luck with Traci's Kid's. From Traci's Dad.*

The tears started again. More than three months ago she waited in a borrowed suite of rooms with Jim, Linda Amanski, and both families. They waited for Uncle Skip to return from the crash site. When he arrived, he brought the inevitable news. There were no survivors. He had wanted to spare her the details, but she insisted. The pain on Uncle Skip's face was terrible but, gradually, he relayed everything he learned from the investigators at the scene. Thinking back, she realized it must have been harder for him than for the rest of them.

The next few days had a surreal feeling as she made plans for a funeral instead of celebrating her wedding. In reality Linda and Jim did all the planning. God, what would I have done without Linda, she thought. Someday she would sit down and tell her how much her help meant during those first few weeks. And Jim. My hero. So strong. He carried me through. He never left my side. I couldn't have made it without them.

The press descended on them like a swarm of locusts, but Uncle Skip took care of them and every thing else to do with the investigation.

She knew all her life that her parents were special people. At the funeral, she found out that those who knew them felt the same way. Friends from their teenage days to the present were there. Business associates came from as far away as Europe. Everyone told her it was a beautiful tribute but, for Traci, it was all a blur. One day before what would have been the happiest day of her life, she lost her whole family. She had to endure the pain of a funeral twice; once for her parent, and once for Chris and Amy. Nothing in life prepares someone to bury their family. People send flowers and cards and wish you the best, but she was numb to their words. Her memories of those days were vague except for the recurring vision of four caskets.

She returned to Tucson after spending three weeks in Connecticut putting her family's affairs in order. That first weekend at home, her grief settled in. Traci didn't know what to do or how to act. She stayed home for almost two months while Fran ran the daycare. The tears flowed daily, and she realized she had to do something. Finally she called Fran and told her she was returning to work.

She closed her eyes and clutched her dad's gift to her chest. I have to get past this, she thought. She sat up and pressed the intercom button.

"Fran, I have to start somewhere. Can you get the time sheets and payroll book for me?"

"Are you sure, Traci? I can do it," Fran replied.

"Thanks, but I need to get busy."

She released the button and looked at the stack of cards. She would open and answer them tonight. It was another thing she had put off for too long. She put the cards in her bag but left the gift from her dad on her desk where she could see it.

Chapter 42

The view from Skip Amanski's office was spectacular. The SKIPCAL CORPORATION'S main offices were located in the financial district of the Lower East Side of Manhattan. The building sat on the corner of Broad Street and Market Field, just two blocks from the New York Stock Exchange. Skip stood looking out across Battery Park to the Statue of Liberty and Ellis Island. The sights and sounds of the harbor never got old for him, and he made it a point each day to spend a few minutes watching from his hidden perch.

He had been back to work for two months now, but he still found it hard to get started each day. Earlier he asked Lois to hold all calls except for an emergency. He knew he could count on Lois; she had been his secretary for ten years.

The only call she put through was from Linda. She called from Washington D.C. to check on him. Linda was acting as a chaperone on a field trip to the Capitol with Ben's high school class. He told her he was fine, but that was a lie. He would never be fine again. For the last twenty years of his life, he had seen or talked to Cal almost every day. Whenever he thought of the things he loved in life—family, laughter, friends, sports, or even just having a couple of beers, he thought of Cal. Now, he was gone. Every half hour or so he went back to the window and watched the ferries make the trip back and forth to Ellis Island. Each time his mind would drift back three months to the morning at the crash site.

Between midnight and six in the morning, he had never really moved except to alternate between standing and sitting. He had watched as the search unfolded. Years of experience allowed him to stay at a distance and still understand the subtleties of what was happening before him. Early on he recognized that one section of the site had been set aside for the remains of victims. A lone police officer was stationed there, and workers came and went with a certain reverence. Then, there were the body bags. Five of them now, lying in an even row under the glow of the searchlights.

Across the clearing, two men with FAA emblazoned on the back of their jackets stood guarding a table. There had been some shouting from the debris, and two men came forward carrying an object. Investigators gathered for a few minutes. When they returned to their work, they left the two men to stand by the table. Skip assumed the object was one of the plane's black boxes.

He was working on his third cup of coffee when two men started toward him. He recognized Tom Anderson, but the other man was a stranger.

"Mr. Amanski, this is Richard Welsh. He is with the FAA, and he is the chief investigator. Dick, this is Mr. Skip Amanski," Anderson said.

"I'm sorry we have to meet on an occasion such as this, Mr. Amanski. You have my deepest sympathy," Welsh said.

"Thank you," Skip replied, extending his hand.

"I'm not sure how much there is to tell right now, but Tom told me that you wanted to be kept informed," Welsh said.

"I would appreciate any information you might have," Skip said.

Welsh took a deep breath and began. "As far as the crash itself, it may be awhile before we can determine why the plane hit the mountain. There was no dive in progress at the time of impact. According to eyewitnesses, the plane flew straight into the side of the mountain. If there is any good news on a night like this, it is that both black boxes have been recovered. One, hopefully, will tell us if there was a mechanical failure, and the other should have recorded voices in the cockpit," Welsh said. He hesitated before going on.

"We believe we have found the remains of five people in the debris. Three men and two women. Would that be an accurate account of the people believed to be on board?"

Skip had known for hours that his friends were dead, but confirmation left a heavy feeling. "Yes. That's right. Five, including the pilot," he whispered.

"Mr. Amanski, we have found certain things that may help in identification. Do you think you are up to it?" Anderson asked.

Skip took a deep breath. "Yes. I can identify all of them. Let's do this now," he answered.

"I'm not sure you understand, Mr. Amanski." You would not be able to recognize them now, but we have uncovered certain items that may help us to identify each individual. We were hoping you could help us in that area," Welsh said gently before continuing. "We believe one man was in the cockpit, and the other four passengers were strapped in their seats. You have to understand that when this plane hit that rock face, the cockpit virtually disintegrated. There is not much left of whoever was in there. The others were not much better off. Look, everyone on this plane died instantly. They never felt the explosion or the ensuing fire, if that is any consolation."

Skip felt nauseous but forced himself to reply. "What did you mean by items you found and how I can help?"

"We have found various items with name tags, partially melted credit cards, and picture ID's." At that point, Welsh pulled a notebook from his pocket and flipped to the page he wanted.

"The items we found lead us to believe that the people on board were as follows: William Cannon, Calvin Mitchell, Janice Mitchell, Christopher Mitchell, and Amy Beth Mitchell. There are some questions, along with where we found certain items that may help us with identification of each individual." Welsh's eyes held Skip's for a moment.

Skip knew what the man was trying to tell him. He would not be asked to identify any bodies. No autopsies would be necessary to determine cause of death—only if they could not determine which body was which. There would be no open caskets.

"How can I help Mr. Welsh?" Skip asked.

"One of the women was blonde?" Welsh asked.

Skip squeezed his eyes shut for a moment, thinking of Amy. Bright blue eyes and shiny golden hair to go with her beautiful smile. He couldn't think of a time when she wasn't smiling.

"Yes. Amy, Chris's wife—Cal and Jan's daughter-in-law. Jan's hair was dark, kind of reddish," he said, softly.

"Thank you. That is all we need to identify the woman. As for the men, it may have taken care of itself, but we need to be sure," Welsh said, looking again at his notebook.

We believe William Cannon was flying the plane when it crashed. Part of his wallet with a credit card was found in the cockpit area. The only question left concerns Calvin Mitchell and his son. One of the men had a wallet and wore a wedding ring. The problem is that the contents of the wallet were destroyed," Welsh said.

The two airline officials looked at each other as Skip laughed. He had listened in amusement many times as Cal tried to explain to Jan why he never wore his wedding ring.

"Cal hasn't worn his wedding ring in almost thirty years," he told them. "Not since the first year they were married. He always claimed he was afraid of losing it. Jan and I always gave him a hard time." By the time Skip finished the sentence, his laughter turned to sadness. "Chris would have worn his ring. Does that help?" he asked.

'Yes. That should clear everything up. I'm sorry I had to put you through this, Mr. Amanski, but it will speed things up," Welsh answered.

"If we are finished, I need to return to my family. They are waiting to hear what you have just told me. I appreciate the respect that you have shown," Skip said. "I will make all arrangements to bring my friends home. I would like to do that as soon as possible. I hope there won't be any delays. Thank you, both."

Skip shook hands with both men and turned to start down the mountain. He hoped Traci would not ask him for details, but he knew that she would.

Now, back in New York, he thought about Traci. He tried to get her to stay with them for a while longer, but she insisted that it was time to go home. She also insisted on being out front for all the funeral services. For the first time, he realized just how much like her mother Traci was. His thoughts were interrupted by the buzz of the intercom.

"I'm sorry to bother you, Mr. Amanski, but your daughter is here to see you," Lois said.

Skip stared at the machine for a moment. What was Michelle doing here? She had returned to Penn State to meet with her counselor about courses she would need to enter medical school in the fall.

Pressing the talk button, he asked, "Michelle is here?"

"No, sir. It's not Michelle. Kerry is here to see you," Lois replied. Cal was incredulous. Kerry was in school out on the Island. He had dropped her off himself that morning.

"Kerry! Is she alone? Never mind, Lois. I'm coming out."

The main reason Skip was against Kerry dating at the age of fourteen was the fact that she looked and carried herself like a twenty year old. Her self-assured, confident attitude made her seem very mature for her age. When Skip stepped into his outer office, he saw none of those qualities. She looked nervous and scared. His first thought was how selfish he had been. Through this whole tragedy, maybe he hadn't paid enough attention to how the kids were being affected. Cal and Jan had been like second parents, and the kids had been like brothers and sisters. Kerry stood twisting a piece of paper in her hands as he stepped into the room. Her eyes were wide, and she looked as if she could cry at any moment.

"What's wrong, kiddo? What are you doing here?" he asked, as he put his big arm around her shoulder.

Kerry looked around the room, stopping to stare at Lois for a moment before looking up into her dad's face. "Can we go in your office, Dad?" she whispered. He knew his kids pretty well, and something was eating at Kerry. He was almost afraid to find out what, but he took her hand and led her to his office door.

"Lois, please hold all calls unless it's my wife."

"Yes, sir," she said, as the office door closed behind them.

Inside, Skip turned Kerry to him with a hand on each shoulder. "Kerry, when I left you at school, everything seemed fine. Why are you here, and how did you get here?"

"I told them at school that I was sick and asked them to call the driver service. You guys gave them the number in case you weren't available to pick me up. When I got in the car, I told him I wanted to come here. I charged it to you, but I tipped him. Please don't be mad. I didn't know what else to do. Mom's still away with Ben on that field trip with the honor students, so I had to come here." Kerry blurted it all out so fast Skip could hardly understand her.

"Whoa! Take it easy, kiddo. I'm not mad, but why did you leave school and come here?" he asked.

Kerry stepped back and unfolded the paper she was holding. Her hands were shaking as she held it out to him. Her voice quivered as she spoke.

"I think Uncle Cal is alive."

Chapter 43

Detective Martini read his handiwork one more time, checking for spelling or grammatical errors. The report involved two suspects arrested the night before in connection with a string of apartment break-ins on the Upper East Side. As he typed his name at the end of the page, the department door banged open.

Phil Markey of the Missing Persons Bureau was known for making a grand entrance, and today was no different. Waving a piece of paper over his head, he shouted, "Hey! Any of you guys know who this guy is? I know I've seen him before, but I can't remember where."

Collins, whose desk was closest to the door, grabbed the paper and looked it over. Handing it back, he said, "Yeah, you dope. It's that Mitchell guy. You know, the millionaire who crashed his plane into a mountain out in Arizona. You've only seen his face a thousand times on TV in the last couple of months.

"Proves how much you know. That guy is dead and buried. This picture was taken three days ago and sent out yesterday," Markey sneered.

Martini was only half listening. He had put the Sullivan case aside as a dead end months ago, but it was never far from his thoughts. Now, slowly, a scenario started to form in the back of his mind.

Mitchell's plane originated in New York. Sullivan disappeared from Kennedy around the same time. His mind raced as he rifled through his desk, searching for the Sullivan file. His chair made a screeching sound and clattered to the floor as he bolted from it, crossing the room in two steps.

"Give me that!" he said, ripping the paper from Markey's hand. The man in the picture sure looked like the guy he had seen all over the news outlets. Martini quickly read the report under the picture.

Male Caucasian, 6'1", two hundred and twenty pounds. Found Friday, October 16 at approximately 7:00 P.M., CST, eighty miles west of Midland,

115

Texas. A rancher found the man on Culverton Ridge. He was wearing blue gym shorts, a gray T-shirt, and a ski jacket. He was also strapped into a parachute harness. The man had been shot twice, once in the upper right chest and once in the head. The man is suffering from a case of amnesia, caused in all likelihood by the head wound. He is expected to recover fully from all other injuries, but the doctors will not speculate on the length of the amnesia. If you know this man, please contact Detective Lowery of the Midland Texas Police Department.

"Frank. What's up? You look like you've seen a ghost," Collins said.

"It's Sullivan. This is how they got out," he muttered. "They disappeared from Kennedy the same day this guy left Kennedy. The same day his plane slammed into a mountain, killing him and everyone else on board. Only problem is, he isn't dead. Instead, he shows up in a Texas hospital with two gunshot wounds and, when they find him, he's wearing a parachute."

Martini stopped and shook his head as other detectives started to gather around him.

"The reports said all passengers were accounted for, which means someone made it look legit to throw off investigators. This has Michael Sullivan written all over it. He hijacked a plane and flew out of here. Why didn't I think of that?" he nearly shouted.

Markey wasn't convinced. "But Frank, if you're right, how did this guy stay missing for so long?" he asked.

"I don't know. Maybe because no one is looking for him. Remember, his body was accounted for in the crash," Martini muttered.

"It doesn't matter now," he said, as he started barking orders. "Collins, get this Detective Lowery guy on the phone. He's with the Midland Texas Police Department. Anybody remember the name of that guy with the SKIPCAL Corporation? The one who answered all the questions on TV for the Mitchell family? I need to talk to him. Somebody find out how we go about getting a body exhumed in the state of Connecticut. We need autopsies. If this guy isn't buried up there, we need to know who is."

Martini held Cal's picture high over his head for everyone to see.

Chapter 44

It had taken them two full days to reach Lake Tahoe. They traveled up the coast, trying to attract as little attention as possible. Once there, they rented a townhouse built into the mountainside. The place was fully furnished except for a computer which Sully purchased that same day.

Twenty-four hours later, Bo arrived in the resort village. After landing in the desert about ten miles from the nearest town, he used an area map and compass to walk out. He then boarded a westbound bus. Arriving in Tahoe, he waited until 10:00 A.M. before heading for the post office. Donna was there waiting. The plan called for Donna to purchase a post office box the first day she and Sully arrived and then, to check it each day at that same time until Bo showed.

Three months later Sully sat and stared at the face on his computer screen. The same face he stared at for a moment in the aisle of that damn plane. The guy snapped Kann's neck like a twig, but he didn't shoot the guy for killing Kann. He shot him because of the danger he saw in the man's eyes. Sully checked all of the news sources coming out of Midland, Texas, twice a day. Bo and Donna kept telling him that he was crazy, but he couldn't rest knowing the man he shot was still out there. Today he was right there on the front page of the Midland paper. The same face except for the dark scar on his forehead and a blank look in his eyes.

"You bastard, you should be dead," Sully whispered to the face on the screen.

Actually he had seen the man a third time. The day they rented the townhouse, Sully hooked up the computer and started searching the Internet. He knew only one man could identify them, and he had to know if the man survived. The safest way to get information was to get online and find a news source. Right away he knew he was dealing with much more than a missing person. The front page of every paper carried the continuing story of a devastating plane crash that killed one of the richest families in the country. The story read that Calvin and Janice Mitchell, traveling to Tucson, Arizona, along with their son and daughter-in-law, died in a terrible accident. The private plane they were traveling in had crashed in Arizona, leaving no survivors. Tragically, they were traveling to the wedding of their only other child, Traci Mitchell, of Tucson, when the tragedy occurred. The pilot, William Cannon, also died in the accident. His wife and two children in Deer Park, Long Island, survived him. The financial world was already in an uproar over what would happen to Mitchell's half of the very successful SKIPCAL CORPORATION.

The next day the first four pages of the paper were devoted to the Mitchell crash. On page five, in the lower left hand corner, under a three by four picture, he found what they had been hoping to avoid. The picture, itself, was useless. It was black and white and very grainy. The left side of the man's face was swollen and bruised. Sully wouldn't have recognized the face if he weren't looking for the story. The report gave all the details of the rescue and the injuries ending with the amnesia diagnosis and asking for help in identifying him. They had known it was possible, but not likely, that the man would survive.

"Shot in the chest and the head, then thrown out of a plane. How do you survive that?" Donna wanted to know at the time.

"He was a tough one, I could tell from the start. But I figured him dead, too," Sully said.

"What's amnesia? That the one where you don't know who you are?" Donna asked.

"That's the one," Sully answered. "I'm not sure what that means to us, but it buys us more time."

They had already changed their names and appearances. On the way up the coast, Sully stopped to see an old acquaintance who fixed them up with false ID's. Bo shaved his head and mustache and was sporting an earring. Donna changed her hair from blonde to black and cut it very short. Sully cut his shoulder length hair to a crew cut and bleached it almost white. All three were wearing new clothes that fit with the style of the young, hip neighborhood they had moved into.

Sully read the news report about Cal. He told himself that all hell would break loose as soon as someone recognized him. The good news was that the guy still had amnesia and may never come out of it. Until he did, no one could link them to the plane. He thought he heard once that the longer someone had amnesia, the less chance they had of recovery. Wishful thinking, he thought to himself. He sat at the computer for a long time, looking at the man he shot. No matter what, the man on the screen was the only person outside of Sully's group who could put them on that plane. The longer he looked, the more his hatred built for the man whose image stared back at him.

Chapter 45

Skip knew the face in the picture. The scar on the forehead was new—and he looked confused, but the man in the picture was Cal.

"Where did you get this, Kerry?" Skip asked.

On the way into the city, she had gone over the events of the day more than once. She began again, to make sure she got everything straight.

"I have a study hall during second period, and I decided to go to the library to do research on a project for my civics class. We have to write a report on any on-going event in the United States. We decided to report on missing children. I got on a site called "Lost and Found" that was set up for families who have had loved ones disappear. They have chat rooms to help each other cope with their losses. There's information on support groups in each state and law enforcement groups that you can contact," Kerry said.

Skip was frustrated and interrupted.

"Kerry, I don't get the connection."

"Please, Dad, I'm almost there," she pleaded. "The site has these two places you can click on, 'LOST' and 'FOUND'. I clicked on 'LOST' and, as I scrolled down, picture after picture of people who have disappeared came on the screen. I got depressed and tried the 'FOUND' button. On this site, people have been found that don't know who they are for various reasons like mental breakdowns, Alzheimer's, or amnesia. There are more people like that than you would think. Anyway, I started scrolling down, and there was Uncle Cal! It says the picture was taken three days ago. It is him, isn't it, Dad?"

Skip read the paragraph under the picture again. "Yes, Kerry, it's him. Grab a seat, honey, I have some calls to make." He was on a roller coaster of thoughts and emotions as he sat behind his desk. He had a familiar feeling in the pit of his stomach. It was a weak—almost fainting—feeling that came to him at certain times in his life: before big games in high school, at his wedding and the births of his children, and many times on duty with the CIA. Now, the feeling was back. He loved Cal like a brother, and he thought he had lost him.

Now, he was alive. Skip couldn't have asked for a better gift; but who had they buried, and what about the rest of the Mitchell's? There were no autopsies—there was no need. And what happened to the plane? The FAA found no sign of foul play. Both black boxes had been found but offered no clues. The first showed no mechanical problems, and the voice recorder had never been turned on. The investigation had long since ended, and the crash was officially listed as pilot error.

Did the article say Cal was shot and wearing a parachute when they found him? Skip slammed his hand on the table hard enough to make Kerry jump.

"Focus!" he shouted, as he squeezed his eyes shut. A moment later, he opened his eyes and pressed the button on the intercom.

"Lois, cancel anything I have for the next few days. Jim will have to take over for a while. I'll need to talk to him before I leave. I will need two cars from the service: one to go back to Southampton, and one to Kennedy Airport. I will be flying today, when and where I don't know yet," he said into the machine.

"Yes, sir," came Lois's surprised voice. "Sir, a Detective Martini called just a moment ago. He said it was very important that he talk to you as soon as possible."

Skip thought for a moment before answering. He had one call to make before he talked to anyone. "Thanks, Lois. I'll deal with him later."

Skip then called Dick Ireland for the second time in a month. Ireland answered immediately.

"Dick, this is Skip Amanski. I'm going to need the agency's help again. I have a picture here that leads me to believe Cal is alive."

"Skipper, I had my hand on the phone when you called. Seems Cal is very much alive. I just received confirmation from the FBI on a set of fingerprints they ran. The request came from a Detective Sam Lowery in Midland, Texas, trying to track down an amnesia victim. His guy is Calvin R. Mitchell. What can I do to help?" Ireland asked.

"I already have a police officer waiting to talk to me," Skip told him. "This story is going to explode, and I need you to slow the process down. Also, we need to put the wraps on the Midland police. I don't want anyone else to talk to Cal before I can get to him. How are your contacts in Texas?"

"I think we can get something done on that front. As far as the story getting out, we can't stop it, but I think I can put out something to divert attention for awhile. Anything else I can do?" Ireland asked.

"Yeah, Dick, a couple of things. I have to know who we buried if it wasn't Cal, and I don't have time to get Traci Mitchell's permission or to go through proper channels. I want to know more than the locals when I get to Texas. Also, I need a home phone number or cell phone number for a James Bradley or Bradley Construction Company in Tucson, Arizona.

"Consider it done, Skip. I'll call you back with the numbers in a few minutes. The rest I'll have for you within twenty-four hours. I'll stay in touch," Ireland promised.

"Thanks, Dick. As soon as I have those numbers, I'll contact Cal's daughter."

Kerry was staring at him when he hung up the phone. She had watched in amazement as he took control of the situation.

"Kerry, I'm sending you home. You'll stay next door at the Allen's until Ben and Mom get home tonight. I will call her in a few minutes to let her know what happened, and then I'll call Mrs. Allen."

He turned back to the intercom and asked, "Lois, how long before the cars arrive?"

"They said a half hour, sir. That was fifteen minutes ago," Lois answered.

"Fifteen minutes? Good. Can you get the police officer on the phone for me now? Thanks, Lois." As he hung up the phone, he looked at his daughter. She looked small with her head bowed, sitting in the chair, wringing her hands. When she raised her eyes, he saw tears and confusion.

He stood and motioned to her. "Come wait with me by the window, kiddo. I don't think you've ever seen the view from here."

Chapter 46

Detective Martini closed the file folder on his lap and looked across the aisle of the Lear jet at Skip Amanski. The private plane and the Lincoln Towne Car did not impress him. During his career, he had to deal with all kinds of people, from the homeless to millionaires. Some of them were victims, some criminals, and some were just pieces of the puzzle on a given case. This guy was no different. His wealth meant nothing to Martini. What did impress him was the fact that this guy was connected and connected like no one he had ever dealt with. It started two hours ago with their phone conversation.

"Detective Martini? My name is Skip Amanski. I am returning your call."

"Thank you, Mr. Amanski. I'm calling about the plane crash that involved your partner, Calvin Mitchell, and his family. I think I may have some news for you in regards to that tragic event," Martini offered.

"I have just seen a picture taken two days ago that leads me to believe that Cal may still be alive," Skip answered.

Skip's statement put the detective on the defensive; a position he did not like and was unaccustomed to.

"I have seen the same picture. We believe that the Mitchell family may have been the victims of a hi-jacking. We had a group of people believed to be involved in a drug deal under surveillance. Somehow they eluded us and, until now, we could not figure out how they got out of Kennedy Airport undetected. We now believe they took your friends and their plane at gunpoint. Can you tell me how you came by the picture, Mr. Amanski?"

"That's not important, detective. What is important is where we go from here. Also, I would like to know more about the people involved in the hi-jacking."

Martini leaned back in his seat. During the phone call that had taken place two hours ago, Amanski made two things clear. His partner would not have been involved in anything illegal and, whether he was injured or not, there was no way he left that plane on his own accord if his family was still alive. That was all well and good, but Martini wasn't even sure at this point that Amanski, himself, wasn't a suspect.

He told Amanski that he had already spoken to a Detective Lowery in Midland and confirmed that there had been no change in the condition of the man thought to be Cal Mitchell. Martini also informed him that because Mitchell was obviously alive, the police would need to exhume the graves in Connecticut to determine who was buried there, and that he would fly to Texas to see Calvin Mitchell in person. Arrangements were being made as they spoke.

Amanski was a cool customer. Nothing Martini said seemed to phase or surprise him. He was leaving within the hour, and Detective Martini was welcome to fly with him. He had a private jet waiting at Kennedy Airport to take him to Midland. Martini thanked him but politely refused.

One hour later, a Lincoln Towne Car picked him up in front of the station. After hanging up with Amanski, he was busy putting things together for the trip when the boss sent for him. In the office, he was told that he would, in fact, join Skip Amanski on his private plane to Arizona. The order came from higher up, and there would be no discussion on the matter. He was to cooperate fully with Amanski. He was still in charge of the investigation for now, but that was subject to change without notice if the "powers-that-be" said so. He was still stunned and angry when the car arrived.

Two men were waiting for them at the steps of the plane when they arrived. The younger of the two men stepped forward, carrying two bags.

"Mr. Amanski, I have the files you requested, along with the portable fax machine. Agent Ireland sends his regards and said for you to stay in touch. As for your other requests, we will forward anything we find as soon as it becomes available."

"Thank you, and thank Agent Ireland for me, please," Skip replied, as he took both bags and turned to the older man.

"My name is Skip Amanski. I'm guessing you're Dr. Franklin?" he said, as he shook the older man's hand.

"That is correct, Mr. Amanski. I have been anxious to meet you. It is not often I am called away from Washington at the drop of a hat," the man said with a touch of admiration in his voice.

"I would be more comfortable if both of you would call me Skip, and I am sorry for the inconvenience, Doctor. Your help in this matter is invaluable and greatly appreciated. I would like to introduce you to Detective Martini of the New York City Police Department. Detective, this is Dr. Howard Franklin, Chief of Neurology at Bethesda Naval Hospital in Washington, D.C.," Skip said, as he introduced the two men. As soon as they were done shaking hands, Skip started up the steps.

"We can talk on the plane. The sooner we are in the air, the better," he said.

On the plane, Dr. Franklin explained all the possible scenarios involved with an amnesia victim, given that he had not yet seen the patient.

That was two hours ago. Martini finished reading the last of five files that Skip handed to him. The first had been a complete dossier on the lives of Calvin Mitchell and his family. Martini realized that Skip wanted him to have no doubts about the kind of person that he was about to meet. The other four files were just as thorough. They included histories on Amanski himself, a Mrs. Carrie Douglas, owner of the *Circle R Ranch* in Midland, a Detective Samuel Lowery of the Midland Texas Police Department, and a larger file that included police records and current status reports on all six members of Mike Sullivan's gang.

Martini was disgusted by what he read about Lowery's career and shocked that Amanski knew who was in the gang. On top of that, Amanski's files were more complete than that of his own department. Glancing at Skip again, he noticed that he was reading one last file. For a moment, he tried to think who was involved in this case that hadn't been covered in what he already read. Then, he realized the last file had to be about him.

"I assume that file has my name on it. Getting this information this fast is impressive. Just who do you know, Mr. Amanski?" he asked.

They looked at each other for a moment, but Skip didn't answer. He closed the file with Martini's name on it and handed it to him.

Chapter 47

Traci and Jim stood on the tarmac of the same airport where they had waited to hear the fate of her family three months earlier. Traci's thoughts and emotions were so jumbled that she couldn't focus on any one thing. Uncle Skip had contacted Jim at his work site and Jim had come to her office to tell her that her dad was alive. She was thankful that Skip had decided to let Jim tell her in person. After Jim gave her the news, he called Skip to have him fax the photo of her dad to them. Only then did she let herself believe he could be alive. But if he was alive, then who did they bury and what about the rest of her family? When Uncle Skip called to say he was on his way to take her to her dad, he also told her a story of drug deals and hijackers, of gunshots and parachutes. He told her that her dad was recovering form his wounds on a ranch in Texas and that he had no memory of who he was. He had amnesia. She watched as the plane taxied toward them knowing only one thing: her dad was live and she had to get to him.

Skip informed those on the plane about the stop in Tucson only after they were in the air. The jet rolled to a stop only a few feet from Jim and Traci. When the steps were lowered, Skip stepped down and went immediately to Traci. He hugged her and shook hands with Jim saying, "Let's go see your dad."

Chapter 48

Sam Lowery sat in the office of Harley Nicolls, Chief of Detectives of the Midland Police Department, and he was not happy. He looked up at the clock. Exactly seven hours since his boss told him that the investigation of Calvin Mitchell was on hold until further notice. There would be no protest on this one. The order came from someone with a lot of power. Lowery would be relegated to desk duty until certain interested parties arrived from New York.

At 8:00 that same morning he was a much happier man. He arrived at work to find more than a hundred communiqués on his desk. All correspondence centered on the photo and fingerprints that he put on the information highway late Friday evening. He had to admit was stunned to find that his amnesia victim was a missing millionaire. The reports were confirmed when a detective Martini called from New York. Martini asked that Lowery wait until his arrival to visit the man again. Lowery had never paid much attention to the coverage of the crash. It wasn't his case and he didn't care about the victims. He of course knew who Calvin Mitchell was and what had happened to him and his family. The story had been everywhere from the crash to the funerals. Now he had the guy holed up on a ranch with a good looking chick. He became more convinced then ever that the guy had been involved in a scam gone wrong and was hiding out. He did not intend to wait for anyone. Mitchell was one of the richest men in the world and Lowery would be more than willing to help him out of a jam for the right price. Just as his plan was formulating, Nicolls lowered the boom.

When the Desk Sergeant called from downstairs to announce the group's arrival, Nicolls went to greet them. Lowery's first thought was to ignore these people. He was sure if there was money to be had in this deal it would be found on the ranch. But what if he were wrong? What if there wasn't a deal gone bad? If he treated the guy's friends right he might at least weasel a reward out of them. He turned his attention to the door opening at the far end of the squad room.

Lowery stood and quickly did a once over of the woman and four men who entered the office with Chief Nicolls. He did not appreciate having his investigation put on hold for anyone, but he would play the good guy role for the time being.

"Detective Lowery, these people just arrived from New York. They are here relative to the Calvin Mitchell amnesia case. This is Miss Traci Mitchell, the daughter of the injured man, and her fiancé, James Bradley," Nicolls said as he introduced the group. "Mr. Skip Amanski, Mr. Mitchell's partner in the SKIPCAL CORPORATION, Dr. Howard Franklin, an amnesia expert from Washington, DC, and Detective Frank Martini. Detective Martini is conducting a drug investigation that may have a connection with this case."

Lowery offered his hand to Traci. "Welcome to Midland, ma'am. I hope we can be of some service to you," he said.

Nicolls hesitated a moment, taken aback by Lowery's polite manner, but then continued. "Mr. Amanski, we are prepared to give you complete authority in this matter as requested. Detective Lowery will take you to the *Circle R Ranch* where Mr. Mitchell is staying as soon as you are ready."

Lowery was seething but kept his cool.

"This case has been pretty cut and dried so far, Chief. It would probably be smoother if I just stayed on top of it and filled them in. Don't you think?"

"It doesn't matter what you or I think. The orders came from Washington. These people are in charge and we will cooperate. Is that clear, Lowery?"

Lowery nodded his head, wondering as he spoke what kind of people had the power to take over a local investigation as quickly as these people had.

"Yes sir. I'll help in whatever way I can."

"We are ready to go as soon as possible. I'm sure you can imagine how anxious Traci is to see her dad." Skip was about to continue when the phone on Nicolls' desk rang.

"Nicolls here," the chief said as he answered the phone. Turning back to the group, he spoke to Martini and then Skip.

"Detective, there is a call for you from your office in New York. You can take that call at my secretary's desk just outside the door. Mr. Amanski, you also have a call, which you can take right here on line two. They didn't say who the call was from."

Skip took the receiver as Martini headed for the office door. Martini kept his eyes on Skip as he listened to Detective Collins back in New York.

"We have come up empty so far on the whereabouts of any member of the gang. None of our contacts across the country have had even a sniff of them. They must be way underground. But we may have found something of interest," Collins reported.

Martini's eyes had not left Skip, who had turned from the others and covered the mouthpiece of the phone he was speaking into.

"Give it to me Pete," Martini said.

"As you know, we have been tracking down all known associates of Mike Sullivan. Well, it may have paid off. In 1985, when he was in the State Pen, Sullivan was buddy buddy with a small time thief named Richie Gomez." Collins paused, and Martini could hear him shuffling papers. "It seems Gomez and his brother, Ron, have surfaced in Miami. The m.o. on these guys is petty crimes, mostly burglary, with the average take in the hundreds. Well, they are throwing around thousands at a time down there, and Richie has been shooting his mouth off about some huge deal."

Martini was listening intently now. "Okay, don't put any heat on them until you hear differently from me. Keep your distance, but also keep tabs on them. If you have contacts who can get close, use them. I want to know more about their big deal. What is the status of the request to search the graves?" he asked.

"I was getting to that. We have been told to back off on that request and, get this Frank, the order came through channels all the way from some bigwig in Washington, DC." Collins replied. For a moment the silence hung in the air. Why am I not surprised, Martini thought?

"I'll be in touch," he said and hung up. The office door opened and Lowery, Dr. Franklin and Chief Nicolls stepped out closing the door behind them.

"What's going on?" Martini asked.

"Amanski asked for a moment alone and I saw no harm," Nicolls answered.

It seemed that Skip Amanski had enough power behind him to get whatever he wanted in this case.

In the office, Skip faced Traci and Jim. Traci had a sinking feeling that he did not have good news.

"I'm sorry, Traci, but I took it upon myself to put things in motion to have the graves exhumed in order to determine the identities of the people buried there. I wanted desperately to get your permission first but I felt it was important to start the process as soon as possible."

"Uncle Skip, I trust your judgment more than you know. You don't have to apologize to me. Was that what the call was about?" As she asked, she took told of Jim's hand and squeezed tight.

Skip took a deep breath. "The pathologist I spoke with is one of the best in the country. Through dental records, they have made positive identifications on all five bodies. Traci, both Chris and Amy died in the crash, but your mom and dad did not."

Traci slowly rose to her feet. Her emotions were as raw as an open wound. She felt the pain of Chris and Amy's death all over again, but also the joy of confirmation that her dad was indeed alive and the sudden realization that her mom might also be alive. It was almost too much to bear. Skip interrupted her thoughts.

"Traci, all the answers we need start with your dad. The sooner we get to him, the better. Let me call them in and tell them what we know. Then we can get going. Okay?"

Ten minutes later, after Skip and Martini shared the information from their separate phone calls, Lowery reluctantly led the group toward the parking garage. He had lost control of the situation and there was nothing he could do about it. He would continue to cooperate and wait for an opening that might benefit him.

Martini was deep in thought. He expected to fight Amanski tooth and nail for leverage in this case, yet Amanski surprised him again. He made it clear to the authorities in Texas that Martini would be in charge of all criminal aspects of the case. Yet he wasn't sure, if push came to shove, where he really stood. He wondered where Amanski got the authority to assign a plane crash in Arizona to a cop from New York. Yet no one was questioning his authority, which meant the power was real. The worst part for Martini was that he was starting to like the guy.

Skip worried about Traci. He knew his own emotions were on a roller coaster ride and he could only imagine what she was going through.

Tom Blenk

Traci walked ahead of the group toward the waiting van. She wiped the tears from her eyes and squared her shoulders. She would deal with her grief later. Her Dad was alive and her Mom might be - that was all that mattered now.

Chapter 49

The van and two tractor trailers parked behind the *Circle R* main barn would be ready to roll by nightfall. They were headed for Topeka, Kansas. The next Professional Bull Riders event was scheduled to start the following Monday. Cal enjoyed the daily work on the ranch and was busy helping to load the last of the livestock. The regular ranch hands came to respect Cal for his hard work and willingness to learn. He loved working with the horses but took a back seat to the wranglers as the animals climbed the ramps. Some went willingly but others were skittish and had a natural fear of the dark enclosed trucks. The horses needed coddling, soothing and sometimes blinders to get the job done. Other stock, such as competition broncs, bulls and cattle, were driven into chutes leading to the respective trucks.

Cal threw the last duffel bag into the van and closed the door. As he walked through the barn, he thought again how comfortable he felt living on the *Circle R Ranch*. Yet he hated that his comfort was tempered by the constant question concerning his identity and what his real life would be like.

Stepping into the compound, he immediately recognized Lowery's jeep parked by the front steps to the main house. A blue van was parked next to the jeep. Cal felt the adrenaline rush through his body. Had Lowery used the pictures and fingerprints to find answers to Cal's real identity? As he reached the front door he noticed the Midland Police insignia stenciled on the van door. He hesitated, thrilled that he might finally get some answers, but worried what secrets they might unlock.

Inside the ranch house opened into a large sunken living room, dominated by a stone fireplace directly opposite the front door.

The next few minutes seemed to pass in slow motion for Cal. Carrie and Detective Lowery were the only people that he recognized in the room. Skip's back was to him, and his form hid Traci from view. He did not see her before he heard her voice.

As her father entered the room, Traci rushed forward. She felt as if her heart would burst as she cried out. "Oh my God, Dad, it is you."

Cal's recognition of his daughter hit him like a physical blow. His eyes shut tight and he felt faint as he staggered, falling against Lowery. Lowery lowered him to the floor in an involuntary motion. Cal's memory flooded back like a fast moving slide show, from his childhood until the present, slowing as it reached the hijacking. A dead man lay at his feet and a gun was pointed at his head. He felt the pain in his chest and forehead. Jan held him and whispered, "Live baby. Just live." As she let go, his scream filled the room.

"No!"

Traci ran to his side. Now, as his eyes opened, she was there in front of him. He grabbed her in his arms and hugged her as tight as he could.

"Dad, you're okay? You know me?"

"Yeah, Honey, I know you." He whispered. He felt weak, but forced himself to ask the only question that mattered to him.

"Traci, where is your mother? What happened to Chris and Amy?" He asked searching her face for an answer. Tears started and she couldn't speak. She looked to Skip for help. He was on a knee next to them and when Traci turned to him, Cal did the same.

"Hey, old buddy, it's good to have you back." Skip said, putting his hand on Cal's shoulder.

Cal searched the face of the man he trusted more than any other.

"Where are they Skip?" He said.

"We need to check you out Cal. We brought the best doctor I could find. First you need to rest and then we can figure out what hap…

The look on his friend's face stopped Skip in full sentence. He knew that look. He had seen it many times and it meant no more bullshit. It meant tell me the truth. He took a deep breath.

"The plane crashed Cal. Chris and Amy were on board. They're dead, but Jan was not on board. We don't know what happened to her. We were hoping you could help us with that.

Cal closed his eyes and his shoulders slumped. His mind reeled as he tried regain his composure, but the news about Chris and Amy hit him hard.

Dr. Franklin watched Cal's transformation with some anxiety. There was no way to tell how long it would take for someone to regain physical or mental capability after such a traumatic event. He worried about a relapse and made his fears known.

"I believe Mr. Mitchell has just suffered his second major traumatic moment in less then three months. These reevaluations could trigger another unpleasant event if we are not careful. First, we need to get Mr. Mitchell up and on the couch. Then I would like to examine him." He said stepping forward. Dr. Franklin did a thorough physical exam and asked a series of questions lasting about a half hour. Finally he stood.

"Remarkably you seem to be doing fine, Mr. Mitchell, both physically and mentally. How much you can handle will be up to you, but I would not recommend that you try to do to much tonight."

Cal sat on the couch with Traci holding his hands. She didn't seem to want to let go and that was fine with him. Skip stood at Cal's side as Detective Martini pulled a chair up in front of them and sat down. He had stayed in the back ground to let the family have some time together, but now it was time for some answers.

"Let me introduce myself, Mr. Mitchell. I am Detective Martini of the New York City Police Department. Maybe we could start in New York City with the hi-jacking if you feel up to it." He said.

For a moment Cal just stared at Martini, but it was as if he was looking through the man. Finally he blinked his eyes and shook his head. He spoke in a subdued voice.

"I stepped out of the shower and they were there, six of them, four men and two woman. They were armed and forced Billy to take off and head for our original destination. They had six or eight bags that they were very protective of. I'm assuming it was a drug deal. The leader, a guy they called Sully, talked about contacting someone in Las Cruces, New Mexico. He was trying to reach a guy named Escala or something like that." Cal stopped for a moment, and before he could continue, Martini spoke.

"Along with your son and daughter-in-law, the remains of the pilot and two other people were found at the scene of the crash. Dental records tell us that the other victims were William Cannon, the pilot, Caitlin Sullivan, Mike Sullivan's sister and James Kann, a small time muscleman from New Jersey. I have a few questions Mr. Mitchell. How did you escape? Do you know what happened to your wife? Do you know how these people died or what caused the plane crash?"

Cal tried to concentrate. Chris and Amy were dead, but Jan might be alive. He had to hold on to that hope.

"I killed the guy from New Jersey. He grabbed Jan and I acted without thinking. If I had kept my cool they all might still be alive. I will never forgive myself for that." Cal paused for a moment. "The guy they called Sully shot me. I don't remember much after that except Jan telling me to stay alive and pushing me out of the plane. That is all I know. When I woke up, I was in a hospital." Cal leaned forward and spoke directly to the man sitting in front of him.

"Now, it's my turn to ask the questions. I want to know everything there is to know about this case Detective."

Before he could answer the beeper on Martini's belt went off and he left the room to find a phone. Skip and Traci tried to fill Cal in on what they knew until he returned.

"That was my office. They have located Larry Webster in Las Vegas. He dyed his hair and grew a mustache, but we have a positive identification. He was one of the men on the plane Mr. Mitchell. We also believe two brothers named Gomez were involved in what we assume was a very large drug deal. Richie Gomez has not been shy about spending money or shooting his mouth off. We had prior knowledge of the deal from Caitlin Sullivan, and I believe her brother found out. I'm sure that's the reason they looked for an alternate route out of New York and why she is dead. As for what happened to your wife, we really have no idea." Martin paused and glanced around the room. He then turned to Cal and asked a question that had been on his mind since their arrival in Texas.

"Am I in charge of this investigation?"

All eyes in the room were on Cal at this point, but all for different reasons.

Traci held Cal's hand hardly able to believe he was really alive.

Carrie sat by the hearth. She did not speak or try to interfere. She knew now that she was in love with Cal. Watching his memory come back created an enormous conflict in her heart. She knew from the beginning that this could happen, but the realization that he belonged to someone else hurt deeply. Still she wanted badly to hold him in her arms and comfort him. She stayed where she was and held back her tears.

Dr. Franklin watched Cal carefully. He found the recovery remarkable. The color returned to his face and his mind seemed alert. He was pretty sure his services would not be needed much longer.

Lowery remained on the landing, watching, waiting and bidding his time. He still believed that there had to be something in all of this for him.

Skip and Cal exchanged glances. No words were necessary. For thirty years they had worked as a team. Cal stood and ran his hands through his hair. He was about to take control.

"Skip trusts you and that is good enough for me. When it comes to arrests or recovery of drugs and money, we will defer to you Detective. As for finding my wife or what that may entail, don't get in my way." Cal spoke quietly, but the tone left no room for argument.

Martini was a smart man. He didn't know who was backing these two men, but he knew they could have him removed from the case in a heartbeat. He wanted Mike Sullivan.

"I have no doubt about who is in charge. I've watched Mr. Amanski operate all day. So be it. I just want this gang in custody." Martini said.

"Good. I am going to Las Cruces. That's where the plane was headed. Skip. You and Detective Martini will have to follow the other two leads. We will need to be able to contact each other directly if any one of us finds information on her whereabouts."

"I will go to Miami. I know Richie Gomez. I know how to push his buttons. If push comes to shove he would sell out his own mother." Martini said. He looked from Cal to Skip and back to Cal. "We will wait for each other before we move on Sullivan, right?"

He was not happy when both men ignored the question.

"That leaves Las Vegas and this guy Webster for me." Skip said. "Mrs. Douglas may I use your phone? I need to make some arrangements."

Lowery started to panic. His chance at a big score was slipping away.

"Hey! What about me? Where do I fit in?" He said. Skip stopped at the door and turned.

"Detective Lowery, you can do us a huge favor by taking Jim, Traci and Dr. Franklin back to town. They will need a room tonight and flights back to their separate destinations when they are ready to go home."

Skip wasn't asking. His tone left no doubt, Lowery was not welcome in the investigation. Lowery fell silent.

"Dad, I want to go with you. I want to be there when you find Mom." Traci pleaded.

"You can't come with me, or any of us, Honey. I'll stay in touch with you through Detective Lowery. It has to be this way, Traci." Cal told her.

Skip returned from his phone call.

"Richard is taking care of all the arrangements. Everything will be ready when we get to the airport. There will be beepers and cell phones waiting in order for us to keep in contact. A helicopter will pick us up in one half-hour." He said.

* * * * *

The jeep and van had pulled out only moments before, and the chopper waited for Cal to board. He stood on the front porch with Carrie.

"I haven't said anything because I'm not sure what I want to say. I owe you my life, but you know it is more than that. I'm not the same guy that fell in love with you. That guy had amnesia, but I can't pretend it didn't happen." Cal paused to looked in her eyes. "I have a wife who I've loved my whole life. I have to find her."

Carrie smiled even as tears filled her eyes.

"I don't think there's any difference between the guy with amnesia and the guy I'm looking at right now. I would want the man I loved to do whatever it took to get me back. Go find her. Time is wasting." She said.

Cal reached and touched her face, letting his fingers linger for a moment. Without a word he turned and walked to the waiting chopper.

Carrie could still feel his touch as the helicopter disappeared in the distance. She was still watching the empty sky when she heard the eighteen wheelers firing up behind the barn. She listened for as moment then turned and went inside to throw some clothes together. She was going to her first rodeo in months. There was no reason to stay on the ranch.

Chapter 50

Lowery sat in his Jeep and watched Dr. Franklin, Traci Mitchell, and her fiancée enter the front door of the Midland Marriott. During the last twenty-four hours, his usual bravado and cockiness had taken a beating. He was now acting as a chauffeur and baby-sitter as his bosses stood by and let some flatfoot from New York take over his case. Worst of all his idea of making some money on this deal was quickly disappearing. Lowery was fuming, but he vowed not to fade away without a fight. He knew Calvin Mitchell was a rich man and, though he never met Mike Sullivan or his gang, he knew they had to walk away from a drug deal like this with plenty of cash. He drummed his fingers on the steering wheel and tried to decide how to funnel the money his way.

Should he follow one of the other three men? No, they didn't give him enough information on where they were going or who they were looking for. He thought about trying to find Sullivan himself but quickly discounted that idea. He stared at the front door of the Marriott again. He made up his mind. The answer was here in Texas with Traci Mitchell or Carrie Douglas. Mitchell would contact his daughter about her mother. He was sure of it. On the other hand, he could not shake the feeling that the Douglas woman and Mitchell were involved in some way. The only remaining question was—stay with the daughter or stay with the girlfriend?

Chapter 51

The man in the photo pinned above the computer seemed to stare back at Sully mockingly. He still believed Mitchell, with his memory intact, was the only person alive who could send him back to jail.

The first picture of Mitchell had surfaced in the Midland news only days after the crash. The picture was fuzzy and didn't connect the man with his true identity. Sully checked every day for three months but, except for a small follow-up, the incident was not mentioned again. The report said the man had amnesia, but Sully was not happy. Then, last Friday, the second picture appeared. This time the photo was clear. It was only a matter of time before he would be recognized. Still, without his memory, he could not hurt them. Sully was nervous. There should have been a media explosion. A supposedly dead millionaire found alive and suffering from amnesia did not happen every day. Yet, forty-eight hours later there was still no follow-up story. It was as if the story never came out. He checked all the major news stories on the net—and still nothing. It made no sense. This was a major story, and no one was talking.

Sully liked being in control. He liked knowing the odds and formulating a plan of action. This situation had definitely gotten out of his control. Was Mitchell alive or dead? Had he regained his memory or not? Were the cops involved? Were they already on their way to Lake Tahoe? These questions and more raced through Sully's head as he paced the room.

He was still pacing when Bo and Donna entered the condo. They had been skiing but returned for a beer and a sandwich. Sully stopped and looked at Bo.

"We need to find out what the hell is going on with this guy, Mitchell."

Chapter 52

Detective Martini watched Richie Gomez through the one-way mirror of an interrogation room in the Miami Police Department building. Richie was the exact opposite of his brother, Ron, whom Martini had spent the last hour interviewing. In the entire sixty minutes, the only time Ron Gomez spoke was to ask for a soda. He gave Martini nothing.

The Gomez brothers were caught virtually with their pants down. They were entertaining two local prostitutes when Martini and members of a Miami swat team broke down the door. The women were released while the men were taken into custody in handcuffs. Ron went quietly while Richie kicked and screamed, demanding to know what the charges were.

An hour and a half later time was starting to wear on Richie. He sat chain smoking in a straight back chair in the center of the room. A chair across the table was the only other piece of furniture in the room. He alternated between slouching back in the chair and sitting up, with his elbows on the table. He strummed his fingers and absently pulled on the chain running from his handcuffs to a metal hook fastened to the chair. No one had spoken to him since his arrival. Richie sat up straight as Martini opened the door.

"Richie, how are you doing today? My name is Detective Martini. I am from New York City, Richie, and I'm here to talk to you about a drug deal between you and Mike Sullivan. We know the deal went down in New Mexico after the plane was hi-jacked. We know that you guys split the money, killed the people onboard, and then crashed the plane. That's murder one, Richie, and your brother says that you set the whole thing up."

Martini loved to go on the offensive with guys like this. Most of it was guess work, but he wanted to push Richie to the edge as fast as possible. His strategy worked. The words tumbled out as Richie leaned halfway across the table.

"Whoa! I don't know what you're talking about," he yelled.

Richie started to sweat. His eyes darted around the room like a couple of ping-pong balls. He fumbled for another cigarette, forgetting that he already had one going.

"We don't need a confession from you, Richie. We already picked up Larry Webster and Robert Boston. Their statements along with Ron's are going to send you to the chair," Martini said. He had not heard any news on either man, but Richie didn't know that.

"Wait! Ronnie is nuts, man. I didn't kill nobody. Sully set the whole thing up with Escalia, and there was never supposed to be no plane," Richie blurted.

"Doesn't matter, Richie. People are dead. Unless someone steps forward and helps us piece this thing together, everyone will pay the same price. Your brother is already talking. If you want to cut a deal, it has to be now."

Richie was scared. He wasn't sure about Ronnie. Would he turn Richie in if they tried to burn him? Webster sure would, and so would Bo. Why take chances? This guy already knew as much as Richie knew himself. He glanced one more time around the room as if searching for a last second escape route. Finally he accepted his fate and said, "What do you want?"

Martini pushed a yellow pad across the table.

"Write down everything you can remember about this deal from day one until today: names, places, phone numbers, and addresses, if you know them. When I say everything, I mean everything, Richie."

An hour later Martini sat in a private office waiting to hear from Skip or Cal. He left voice messages for both after finishing with the Gomez brothers. He now believed he had a clear picture of the entire deal as it unfolded from New York to New Mexico, but he did not have what he came to Miami in search of. He did not know the whereabouts of Mike Sullivan, Robert Boston, or Donna Murry. Most importantly he had no information on Jan Mitchell.

He poured himself another cup of coffee. It was his fifth cup in four hours. I wonder how those guys made out. I hope they got better results than I did, he thought.

Chapter 53

Larry Webster tried to keep a low profile when he arrived in Las Vegas. He changed his appearance, rented a small apartment, and purchased a new wardrobe. He kept his budget at the casinos to no more than a thousand dollars a day, but that routine got old in a hurry. Webster was an addict, and he had a bankroll of one hundred fifty thousand dollars. What was the sense of having that kind of money if you couldn't bet with the big boys? Besides, as far as he could tell, no one suspected foul play in the Arizona crash.

After two months, he moved into a suite at the Mirage at a cost of five hundred dollars a night. He never played the same casino two days in a row. Some days he played one during the day and then, after a meal and a nap, he played a different one at night. His betting pattern changed also. He established a fifty thousand dollar line of credit at the Mirage which he could borrow on at any casino along the strip.

As he stepped off the elevator, he reviewed his current finances in his mind. If his calculations were correct, his bankroll was virtually intact, not counting expenses. His taste in rooms, girls, food, and clothes was expensive. Who cares? he thought. At one point he was down about twenty thousand, but tonight had been a good one. The five thousand he started with grew to twenty before he called it a night, and now he was looking forward to Jennifer. Jennifer was a high priced call girl who would be waiting in his room. She was a regular passion for him on nights when he won big. He called her on his cell phone from the table an hour earlier and then called the front desk to have a key left for her. His excitement grew as his key turned in the door. She knew what he liked, and she would be ready for him.

The living room was dark and quiet as always. He could picture her lying on the bedspread dressed in lingerie and stockings, waiting. He dropped his jacket in a chair and entered the bedroom.

Webster was confused. The bed was empty. He had given her plenty of time to get there ahead of him. The light was on in the bathroom. Maybe she was in there. He took one step toward the door when a voice stopped him and turned his blood cold.

"She's not here, Larry," Skip said.

Webster spun around to face Skip who was sitting in the shadows on the far side of the room. He then glanced at the foot of the bed and tried to judge the distance to his shoulder bag.

"It's not there, so don't bother," Skip said, as he ran his hand over the Bizon Two he had removed from Webster's bag. "This is quite a weapon. I haven't seen one in a long time. Did you build it yourself?"

"Who are you, and what do you want?" Webster stammered, as he searched the room for a way out. He decided on the door and inched his way closer. Skip moved at the same time. Slowly rising, he placed the gun on the chair and stood between Webster and the door.

"It doesn't concern you who I am. What does concern you is what I want. What happened to Jan Mitchell? Where did Mike Sullivan, Robert Boston, and Donna Murry go when they left New Mexico? Neither of us is leaving this room until you give me those answers," Skip said.

Webster was stunned by Skip's questions and started to panic. "I don't know who or what you're talking about," Webster nearly screamed.

"That's the wrong answer, Larry," Skip said, as he stepped toward the other man.

* * * * *

Forty-five minutes later Skip left the room after making a call to hotel security. He left Webster tied and gagged in the middle of the living room floor. When they found him, they would find close to a hundred thousand dollars in cash next to him and a phone number for Detective Collins in New York. The fight was over quickly, but the punishment lasted a while longer. Webster was weak without a weapon and willing to talk, but it took him a while to convince Skip that he didn't know what happened to Jan. Webster's face was swollen, and his right eye was already black and blue. Most of his discomfort in the next few weeks would come from the rib cage area where he had taken the brunt of Skip's fury.

Twice while still in the room, Skip tried to contact Cal but couldn't get an answer. He hoped the phone was out of range or turned off. He didn't want to think of the alternatives. As he entered the elevator, he dialed Martini's number in Miami.

"Martini? Amanski here. They left Jan alive in New Mexico, and Sullivan headed for Lake Tahoe. Yeah. I'm sure. Webster? Yes, I would say he cooperated. Have you heard from Cal? Okay. You better head back here. I'll get a room and wait for you. Hopefully one of us will hear from him by then. I'll see you when you get here."

Skip hung up and pressed the down button. He stared at the number above his head as it changed with each passing floor. The good news was that Jan was alive when the gang left New Mexico, but that was two months ago. A few minutes earlier he came close to killing a man. His anger was fueled by what they did to his friends, but he stopped himself just in time. Now he was worried about Cal; what he might find in Las Cruces and what he might do.

Chapter 54

The sign to the right of the main entrance read *El Club Delanoche*. *The Nightclub*, translated to English, served as the primary social outlet in Las Cruces, New Mexico. Patrons could choose among three very different activities upon arriving at the converted warehouse.

The entrance to the right side of the building led to the top floor which served as a huge shopping mall. This mall was different from most in that it closed during the day and opened at night. The corridors between shops were made of cobblestone walkways and adobe walls. Sidewalk bars and vendors, selling an assortment of Mexican foods, were strategically placed throughout the halls.

The shops were set up to accommodate the various tastes of all visitors. Shoppers could browse the racks to find any American brand name at black market prices or buy authentic Mexican wear next door. Men's suits or formal wear could be purchased or rented. The finest in women's dresses and gowns were in order along with a lingerie shop where sales ladies would willingly model the merchandise. Many of the shops sported trinkets and Spanish artifacts.

Along with the food and drinks, musicians wandered the hallways, making the whole experience festive and enjoyable.

The left entrance opened up a world of excellent dining. Patrons found five restaurants to choose from on the second floor. The most elegant of the five featured a menu that included food from any of the other four eateries. The other restaurants served Mexican, American, Chinese, and French cuisine respectively. People came from far and wide to eat at *El Club Delanoche*. Those that did went away pampered and satisfied.

Many who ate in the restaurants continued their special evening downstairs in one of the nightclubs. The ground floor split into three soundproof rooms. There was an oldie's club to the right, a seventies disco on the left, and a middle room with a decidedly Latino flavor. All three rooms featured bars on each side with strobe lights and oversized circular dance floors. Disc jockeys blared music until four in the morning.

An assortment of people came to the nightclubs—some to watch, some to drink, and some to dance, but there was more to be found here. This was the place to get drugs and women. Juan Escalia owned *El Club Delanoche* until his unexpected death. Now his two younger brothers ran the business. Most of their day-to-day trafficking went on in the three nightclubs.

Cal sat at the corner of a bar in the Latino night spot. He melded easily into the diverse clientele of the club. He had been at *El Club Delanoche* for an hour, watching and waiting. It was 2:00 A.M., and he had focused on a group of Mexicans drinking, snorting coke, and dancing nearby. A man in the group called Miguel seemed to preside over the festivities. Cal turned a little in his seat as Miguel approached the bar.

"Hombre, maybe you can help me?" Cal said, in a low voice.

Miguel was feeling pretty good but still looked him over warily.

"Do I know you, Senor?" he asked.

"No, but let me buy a round for you and your friends, and we can talk. Okay?" Cal said.

"If I said yes, what would we talk about?" Miguel asked, sporting a wide grin. Maybe he could work this guy for more than just a few drinks before the night was out. The club was famous for gringos spending enormous amounts of money for women and drugs, and he wasn't shy about helping them.

"Put his drinks on my tab," Cal said to the bartender.

"My name is Bob, and I have a large amount of stuff to move. I need to find a contact down here," Cal said, extending his hand.

Miguel shook hands and then gave his drink order. "What kind of stuff we talking, man? I know people who can handle almost anything."

"My seller told me to come here and ask for Juan Escalia. Do you know him?" Cal asked.

Miguel laughed loudly and then said, "You are going to have a hard time finding him, my friend. He is dead. Some gringo broad he was trying to bang killed him. Stuck a piece of glass in his neck and let him bleed to death." Miguel turned toward his table. "Carlos, get over here. You will love this," he yelled.

The woman in the man's story was Jan. Cal was sure of it. His face showed no emotion. No one could have guessed that he had a vested interest in the answer.

"The big boss down here is dead, and a woman killed him. That's hard to believe. What happened to the woman?" Cal said. Carlos approached the two men as Cal asked the question. Miguel grinned at him.

"Carlos, the gringo wants to know what happened to the bitch who killed Juan. Why don't you tell him?"

Carlos was instantly angry. He knew where this was going. He had been ridiculed unmercifully for the last month, and he'd had enough.

"Fuck you, Miguel! She killed the boss, and she is dead. That's all that matters. If you know what is good for you, you will drop it and leave me alone," Carlos spit out.

"No, that is not all, my friend. You forget how she tied Enrique up like a roped calf and stabbed you bad enough to put you in the hospital. It was only then that you shot her in the back as she ran away. You always leave out the good parts, Carlos," Miguel said, as he doubled over in laughter.

Cal's features never changed as the two men started arguing loudly. His CIA training allowed him to mask his emotions, and he had never needed that training more than this moment. Neither man noticed the cold rage in his eyes. The pain he felt was like nothing he had ever known. From the moment he regained his memory, he functioned on the belief that he would find Jan alive. Slowly he dragged his mind back to the present. The man who killed Jan stood in front of him. He knew he would kill the man if he didn't get out of there and regroup.

"Hey, guys. I hate to interrupt, but I need to contact my seller and let him know Escalia is dead. I don't know what he will want to do. Where can I reach you if he still wants to do business?" Cal asked Miguel.

Miguel looked him over for a moment as Carlos stormed back to his table.

"I am here most nights, Senor. If you want me, you can find me here. I can put you with the right people," he said.

"I'll be in touch," Cal said. He finished his drink and paid the bill. Cal shook hands with Miguel and made his way through the crowd. No one saw him glance at Carlos, and no one saw the hate in his eyes.

* * * * *

Miguel and Carlos left the club together at 5:00 A.M. The club closed at four, but they both took advantage of the private rooms at their disposal. They preferred to entertain ladies at the club rather than at their condo. They didn't want to deal with hugs, kisses, or good-byes in the morning.

The garages at the condo complex were located between the main buildings. Carlos parked the Jeep and pressed the button to close the garage door. He was closing the Jeep door when he heard Miguel gasp. Miguel did not see Cal before the elbow slammed into the side of his head. The second blow came from Cal's knee knocking him unconscious.

Carlos was on the other side of the Jeep and had time to react as Cal's attention turned to him. Quickly he pulled the switchblade from his pocket. Snapping it open, he yelled, "Coward! You will not have it so easy with me. No sneak attacks. Come, and I will cut you badly, my friend."

Cal moved slowly, sizing up the man in front of him. He learned long ago to make his opponent change focus and make a false move.

"This will be different for you, Carlos. There are no women for you to kill tonight," Cal said, with as much disdain in his voice as he could muster.

He got the reaction he expected. Carlos lunged at him, swearing in Spanish. Cal caught the man's right arm in both of his and snapped it at the elbow. The cracking sound and the scream were simultaneous. Cal grabbed the knife and held the man on his feet. For the second time in his life, Carlos felt the blade dig deep into his body. Only this time, the person with the knife knew what he was doing.

Cal leaned close and whispered in the dying man's ear, "You were a walking dead man the moment you killed my wife."

* * * * *

An hour later Cal was on a plane bound for Lake Tahoe. He waited for Miguel to wake up and threatened the same fate as Carlos if he didn't tell all he knew about the plane, the deal, and the whereabouts of the gang members. Miguel could not talk fast enough as he stared at the body at his feet. When Cal left, he was convinced that Miguel knew nothing.

Drug enforcement officers from Washington sent by Richard Ireland would arrive before dawn to arrest Miguel for murder. His prints would be on the knife, and no one would ever know that he was found tied and gagged. That same day Escalia's home and nightclub would be raided using Ireland's people. The drug cartel of Las Cruces, New Mexico would never be the same.

Cal called Skip as he left the condo and told him about Jan. He almost choked on the words. It seemed so much harder to say the words out loud to Skip than to say them to himself.

He stared straight ahead and thought about seeing Mike Sullivan in person for the second time.

Chapter 55

On the taxi ride back to the condo, Donna thought about the two guys she left at the casino and laughed. Bo loved to play craps and called her his lucky charm. Usually when she went alone, she stuck to the slots, but she loved the excitement at the tables and today decided to try her own luck.

She was at one table for about an hour when Hank and Ted slid in beside her. The boys were drinking steadily, and they were much more interested in her than in the money they were betting. They had no shot of getting what they wanted from her, but Donna loved to tease and played right along. They hovered around her for almost an hour, accidentally leaning against her to place a bet, or brushing her breast to reach for the ashtray. They took turns moving from one side of her to the other, casually rubbing against her as they did. It never failed to amaze her how guys figured if they turned on their own version of charm, that a woman—any woman—should be honored to jump in bed with them. She laughed again as she paid the cab driver. She could still remember the looks on their faces when she told them she had to get home to her husband and kids. The smile was still on her face when she unlocked the door, but it disappeared quickly as she realized she had visitors.

Detective Martini stood by the door, closed it, and stepped behind her. At the same moment, Skip moved from the shadows of the kitchen wall. Donna tried not to panic. She started to ask what they wanted when she saw the third man. She recognized Cal instantly. She had seen his picture pinned on the wall every day for three months. She never expected to see him alive again, and finding him standing in her living room stunned her.

Fear coursed through her as he stepped toward her. The pure hate in his eyes made her blood run cold.

"Where are they?" Cal said, in a voice she would never forget. Donna was not very bright, but she knew enough not to try to fool this man.

"They left last night. They were looking for you," she managed to whisper.

152

The three men stole a glance at each other before Cal spoke again. "What do you mean? Why would they be looking for me?"

"Sully was crazy about you being alive. We both tried to talk him out of going. Bo wanted to leave and go to Mexico, or Canada, or overseas, but Sully wouldn't listen. He kept telling us that you should be dead, and he was going to make sure you never told anyone what happened," she blurted.

"Where did they go? How would they know where to look for me?"

"I'm not sure. Someplace in Texas. They kept talking about a ranch or something that Sully read about on the computer. I didn't pay that much attention. Please don't hurt me!" she said to Cal.

He had continued toward her until her back was against the wall. He was close enough for her to hear him breathe. Cal stayed there for a long moment with the woman cowering in front of him. Finally he turned to Martini and Skip.

"Frank, you need to call someone to take her in. Skip, we need a plane to Midland and a chopper to the ranch." He turned back to Donna who had not moved. "When did you say they left, and how are they getting there?" he asked.

They took the Blazer and left early this morning. I have to take a cab to get anywhere," she said, unhappily.

"We need to get there as fast as possible. Make your calls. I have to warn Carrie," Cal said. He and Skip reached for their cell-phones as Martini grabbed the receiver from the wall-phone and started punching numbers.

Chapter 56

Lowery was like a bulldog when he thought he had an angle, but even he was getting discouraged. Traci had returned to Tucson soon after her father left town. He had been in touch with the Mitchell girl everyday but, so far, had not heard from the father. Still he continued to assure her that as soon as her father called, he would contact her.

In reality Lowery didn't know if Mitchell would get in touch with him at all. Mitchell could have been blowing smoke to shut Lowery up when he said he would keep in touch with his daughter through the detective. He wanted her to trust him, and so he kept calling. If Mitchell called his daughter first, Lowery would go to Tucson to make his move. In the meantime, he kept an around the clock stakeout at the entrance to the *Circle R Ranch*.

Lowery was dozing when he heard the helicopter overhead. An hour later three trucks full of *Circle R* employees left the property. He followed at a safe distance until they stopped at the Midland Marriott. In the lobby, he found the employees checking in. Lowery explained that he was on his way to the ranch when he noticed them pulling into the parking lot and wondered if there was a problem. They were not happy and more than willing to vent. The amnesia guy showed up at the ranch in a helicopter, scaring the hell out of the livestock. He had a New York cop and a guy flashing a CIA badge with him. They told everyone they had to leave until further notice. That was all they knew, but they were glad to see a Midland cop. They were just talking about calling the local police to see if they knew what was going on. Lowery told them to go ahead and check in. He would head out to the ranch and, as soon as he knew something, he would let them know.

As he left the hotel, he dialed Traci's number. Unless he was mistaken, things were about to break.

Chapter 57

The two men had been in the vehicle for almost three days. They stopped for bathroom breaks and food, nothing else. By the time they hit the outskirts of Midland, Bo was more convinced than ever that Sully was crazy. He wasn't far from the truth. Sully was obsessed with Mitchell. Finding and eliminating Cal became a singular mission in his mind. Bo worried most about the chances Sully was taking. It was a bad idea to come to Texas to find a guy who may or may not be able to identify them. It didn't really matter if he had gone to the cops or if he was still out of his head. How were they going to get near him if he was living on a ranch with a bunch of people? Bo still had his doubts as he parked the Blazer in the Burger King parking lot.

The fast food restaurant sat in the center of a mini mall on the west end of the town.

"Hit a few of the stores on that side, I'll check this side. Talk up the idea that you are looking for work on a ranch. The place is called the *Circle R.* Don't mention it by name. We don't want to draw attention to ourselves." Sully paused and looked quickly around the parking lot. "We'll meet back here in an hour."

Sully returned ten minutes ahead of schedule to find Bo already waiting. "What have you got?" he asked, as he opened the passenger door.

"The *Circle R Ranch* is on the other side of town about five miles down the highway. There ain't no signs, but there is an access road. After you come around a sharp curve with a big wall of rocks on your left, there's a road cut between two big boulders." Bo stopped for a second to stuff another handful of French-fries in his mouth before continuing. "Anyway, the guy said to go about five miles. It's the first left we'll come to. It looks like it's your lucky day, Sully. Most of the ranch hands took off to a rodeo somewhere in Kansas two days ago. That pretty much what you got?" Bo asked.

"Yeah, except for the rodeo stuff. Did anyone mention Mitchell?" Sully asked.

"No, and I wasn't about to ask. I didn't want anyone connecting us with him," Bo said.

Tom Blenk

"Okay. Let's go. This guy isn't walking away this time," Sully said, as he checked the Magnum to make sure it was still loaded.

Chapter 58

The access road ran a mile from the highway to the front gate. When Rory Douglas first put the road in, he painstakingly made sure the landscape stayed the same. Accordingly, the trail wound around and through boulders, trees, rocks, and bushes. The buildings on the ranch could not be seen from the trail until the gate came into view.

Bo maneuvered the Blazer slowly along the road, stopping a few times to make sure no one was coming from the other direction. Finally they reached the main gate. The gate did not exist to keep anyone in or out. It consisted of two fifteen-foot high wooden beams, each one supported on the outside by a large boulder. A collection of beams across the top completed the structure with the ranch's name, C I R C L E - R, framed in the middle.

Bo parked the truck behind a boulder and got out, pulling the Beretta from his belt. Sully held the Magnum in his lap from the time they started down the road. Now he stood with it at his side and stared out at the group of buildings in front of him.

"It looks like a ghost town," he said.

"Let's get out of here while we still can, Sully. This guy might not even be here," Bo pleaded.

"We're staying. If he's gone, someone will know where he went. If no one's here, we'll wait." Sully retorted.

They could see no signs of life except for horses in a corral behind the barn. The two men slipped from behind the rocks and sprinted to separate corners of the bunkhouse. They kept a covering fire over each other as they searched each structure. As they moved from the bunkhouse to the guest houses, they kept a watchful eye on the main house across the compound.

Bo reached the barn door first, with Sully five steps behind. Sully glanced again at the main house. As he did, Cal stepped from the small tack room next to the barn and pressed the barrel of his gun against Sully's temple.

"Remember me?" Cal spat.

When Cal spoke Bo whirled to help but, before he could bring the Beretta up, he heard Skip behind him.

157

"Drop it," Skip said, as he stepped from the barn followed closely by Martini. Bo was not stupid enough to think he could beat these odds. He dropped the gun and raised his hands. Martini quickly pulled Bo's hands behind his back and handcuffed him.

Cal saw none of this. His attention was focused on Mike Sullivan. He ground the barrel into the side of Sully's head.

"Drop the gun or I will blow your head off," he hissed. When the Magnum hit the ground, Cal pushed Sully into the open away from him. He tossed his weapon to Skip and turned back toward Sully.

"You should have left us alone. I offered you more money than you could have gotten from any drug deal. You should have taken the money. Instead, you chose to hurt my family. That was a bad choice," Cal said.

It took Sully a moment to realize that Cal intended to fight him. He relished the thought. He was caught anyway; why not take someone with him? He hated the bastard. If he had just died, none of this would be happening. He knew Cal was tough and skilled from the incident on the plane, but that didn't bother him. He had been in plenty of fights—in and out of prison—and he had killed more than once. Sully was powerful, relentless, and dirty, a lethal combination.

He grinned and started to circle Cal. Suddenly he struck, hitting Cal with three tremendous body shots.

Cal felt the pain shoot through his chest but ignored it. He took two more blows to his ribs in order to move in close. Once there, his hands shot out and grabbed Sully's neck in a vice-like grip. Sully acted in anger and then fear, striking out at Cal's head and ribs.

Cal was oblivious to the pain as he squeezed tighter and tighter. He tried to make his hands meet in the middle. Tried to choke the life out of the man who caused the deaths of people he loved. Sully started to weaken, sinking to his knees, still locked in Cal's grip and slowly dying.

Skip wanted him dead, too. Alone in the hotel in Vegas, he would not have hesitated to kill him, but he would not let his friend do it here in front of witnesses. He would not let Cal go to jail on top of everything else.

Skip had always been the stronger of the two men, but now with his chest against Cal's back, he tried to pry the hands from Sully's neck. The hands and arms felt like iron as he pulled with all his might and shouted in his friend's ear.

"Cal! Stop! Not here. Not like this. Cal! Listen to me. Cal! It's me, Skip."

Cal had only one focus, and something was interrupting—something was interfering and getting louder. He had to deal with it in order to finish. He let go of Sully and turned on Skip with a look of rage that Skip had never seen before. Skip wrapped Cal in a bear hug and screamed in his face, "Cal, snap out of it! It's me."

Somewhere in Cal's mind, his friend's voice clicked. His body went limp, and he looked in Skip's eyes.

"Okay, buddy. I hear you. You can let go now."

Skip had his arm around Cal's shoulder as Sully gasped for breath at their feet. Martini had Bo under guard as they watched the scene unfold. None of them noticed the Jeep enter the main gate. Now everyone but Sully turned as the vehicle approached. The windshield was covered with dirt, but Cal recognized Lowery's Jeep immediately. Lowery got out of the driver's side, and Traci stepped out from the passenger's side.

Lowery called Traci from the hotel twenty-four hours earlier. He told her that her dad was returning to the ranch, and he wanted her to meet him there. Lowery didn't have any details, but her father had information on her mother. Her dad wanted to tell her in person.

Traci left ten minutes after receiving the call and was on the next plane to Midland. She called Jim from the car. He begged her to wait for him, but she wouldn't listen. She would call him as soon as she learned anything. Lowery met her at the airport three hours later and drove her directly to the ranch. He didn't need much of a story to distract her. She only wanted to get to her father and find out about her mother.

Now as Traci moved in front of the Jeep toward Cal, Lowery stepped behind her, wrapped one arm around her neck, and pointed his gun at her head.

"That's close enough, Dad." he said.

Cal had started to go to Traci when he first saw her, but now he stopped where he was.

Martini was the first person to speak. "What the hell do you think you're doing, Lowery?"

"Shut up and drop the guns. I'm taking care of Sam Lowery for once. I'm coming out of this with cash, and I mean a lot of cash," Lowery said, as he swung the gun from one person to another.

"You guys wanted to cut me out. Well, I'm guessing these guys might feel different. Now drop the guns. I won't tell you again," he demanded.

Martini looked to Skip—who dropped his gun—and nodded. Martini tossed his gun toward Lowery who kicked it aside.

"These guys can't give you the kind of money that I can. Let my daughter go, and I will make you rich," Cal said.

"Forget it. My deal is with them, Lowery said, pointing to Sully and Bo. They're a lot less likely to send people after me, and I don't expect they will be leaving too many witnesses. This way, I won't be dodging the police the rest of my life."

The commotion around the Jeep gave Sully time to recover. He felt like he was swallowing razor blades as he started to focus on what was happening. He saw the Magnum lying on the ground a few feet away. Slowly, he rolled once—and then again. When he stood, he had the weapon hidden by his side.

No one noticed Sully's movements except Lowery. He decided to make his pitch right away. If the guy didn't like it, he still had a gun and the girl as protection.

"Hey, partner, the name is Sam, and I'm the guy who came to your rescue. All I want is a good cut of what you guys got for the drugs, and I'll be gone. You can do what you want with them. I really don't care," he said with a grin.

Sully raised the Magnum and shot Lowery between the eyes. The blood splattered on Traci, and she screamed as they both fell. Lowery was dead before he hit the ground. Traci started to scramble away, but Sully's voice stopped her.

"Don't move another inch lady, and if anyone else moves, I'll kill her next," he said, in a voice that croaked with pain. Cal was the closest to Sully, but not close enough to get to him before he could shoot Traci.

"Bo, kick those guns over by the Jeep. The rest of you, get over by the barn door," Sully said. Bo couldn't believe they were going to get out of this and jumped to do as he was told. Traci stood and went to

Cal's side. Cal hugged her and started to move toward the barn where Skip and Detective Martini were standing.

As they started to move, Sully spoke again. Waving the gun at Cal, he said, "Not you. We have some unfinished business."

Cal stopped and faced Sully. He knew there was a good chance he could die, but he would hold Sully's attention long enough for Skip to get a gun. No one else that he loved was going to die at this man's hands. He took a quick look at Skip and knew his old friend understood and would be ready.

"Sully, get the keys and get me out of these things," Bo begged.

"Shut up," Sully said, without taking his eyes off Cal. "You should have died on that plane. It would have saved all of us a lot of trouble. Now a lot of other people are going to die, too. But—you first. I won't leave the job unfinished this time," he spat out.

"You're nothing but a small time hood. The reason I'm alive and the reason you'll never get to spend that money is that my wife was smarter than you," Cal said, laughing and inching closer. "She got me off that plane and made a fool of you. Even if you get out of here, every cop in the United States will be after you tomorrow."

Sully hated the man in front of him. He knew what Cal said was true, but if he had just died like any other man, Sully would be living it up in Tahoe. Well, it was time for payback, he thought, as he pointed the gun at Cal's head. "Maybe so, pal, but you won't be around to read about it," Sully said.

The shot rang out, and it was hard to tell who was more shocked, Cal or Sully. Traci screamed, and Skip started forward but stopped after two steps. Cal flinched and reached for his forehead in a reflex action. Sully stared at the gun in his hand as he fell to his knees. He was confused; his mind couldn't understand how he had been shot. He looked down and saw the blood seeping from his shirt. He searched Cal's face for an answer but saw nothing but hate as he fell on his face.

The realization that the shot came from the area of the ranch house seemed to hit them all at the same time. They turned to see Carrie standing high in Spider's stirrups, still looking down the barrel of her Winchester.

Tom Blenk

Epilogue

It was autumn again in New York. The leaves were already falling and the air had a cool, crisp smell. Cal always loved the fall; it reminded him of football games and younger days. This year was different. Things had changed forever. He sat in his office overlooking the Hudson River and thought back on the events of the last year. A lot had taken place.

The Midland police waived extradition of Robert Boston, and he was returned to New York. The trials and appeals took nearly six months with Donna Murray, Larry Webster, and the Gomez brothers falling all over each other trying to cut deals. In the end, Boston was convicted of four counts of murder, along with various other charges ranging from kidnapping to drug trafficking. He was serving multiple life sentences at Rikers Island with no chance of parole. The other four were serving varying sentences in institutions throughout New York. Donna Murray got off the lightest by giving state's evidence, but even she would not see the outside of a prison wall for a very long time. Cal gave depositions but did not attend any of the trials.

There were a number of accolades awaiting Detective Frank Martini when he returned to the city. The mayor and police commissioner set up a press conference at which time Martini was supposed to receive the city's highest service award. He was also asked to answer questions about the Mitchell case. Martini refused the award, saying he had a small part in the investigation. He also refused to answer questions about the case, referring the press to his superiors. He told them he was a cop, not a politician. At 6:00 A.M. the next morning, Detective Martini sat at his desk, took a sip of coffee, lit a cigarette, and opened the top file of unsolved crimes that sat on his desk. For him, the Mitchell case was closed.

In Midland and Las Vegas, a complete and thorough investigation was conducted concerning the activities and career of Detective Sam Lowery. Both police departments wanted to distance themselves from him as fast as possible. All of his past actions were brought out in the open, including his implication in the murder of a Las Vegas hooker.

Neither police department commented on how a guy like Lowery had remained a cop for so long.

Miguel Santiago had the good sense to cooperate from a New Mexico jail by divulging the whereabouts of Jan's grave. Experts determined that the remains were, in fact, those of Jan Mitchell. Cal brought her home and buried her beside Chris and Amy in a small private ceremony that included Cal, Traci and Jim, Skip, Linda, and their children. With their help, he put his home up for sale and stored all of the family belongings. The first offer came in less than a month, and Cal took it. He had been living in the company apartment in Manhattan ever since.

He kept busy during the early months dealing with Jan's affairs. He met with the branch managers of SKETCHES and made each one a minority partner and doubled their salaries. He instructed them that the name would be changed to SKETCHES BY JAN. A percentage of all profits would go in a trust from each store to its individual majority owner. The new owners would be Kerry Amanski in New York, Ben Amanski in Chicago, Michelle Amanski in San Francisco, and Traci Mitchell Bradley in Paris. If any one of them ever wanted to take over the day-to-day operations, that would be their right. Until then, things would continue as they were. All other belongings and assets were turned over or put in Traci's name. Chris and Amy's possessions went to Amy's parents to do with as they saw fit.

Traci and Jim got married in June in a quiet ceremony in Tucson. It was bittersweet for both of them without Jan but, all in all, it was a great day. Traci and Jim were expecting a child in May. They called to tell Cal just last night.

Cal had not talked to Carrie in person since the day at the ranch when she saved his life for the second time. After the shooting, Martini took charge of Bo Boston and Skip called 911, asking for police and an ambulance to be dispatched to the *Circle R Ranch*. He explained that there had been a shooting with two dead and one prisoner in custody. Traci was nearly hysterical, and Cal immediately took her to the house where Carrie insisted she lay on the couch until she felt better. Carrie was pretty shook up herself with the realization that she had killed a man. It wasn't until later that she was able to explain how she happened to be in the position to help with Mike Sullivan.

The *Circle R* caravan traveled straight through to Topeka, Kansas, stopping only for food and gas. They took care of unloading the stock and found their accommodations that first night. The first two days were always a whirlwind spent in inspections by rodeo officials, paperwork, and care of the animals. It was after things calmed down and everyone was waiting for the competition to start that Carrie realized her heart was not in it. After quite a bit of pleading and cajoling to sway her, the others realized they were not going to change her mind. She was going home. Each one offered to go back with her, but she was going alone and that was that. All hands would be needed at the show to handle the stock, and there was no sense in being short-handed.

After loading Spider in the double horse trailer behind the pickup, Carrie took off, promising to call when she reached the ranch. She stopped twice on the eighteen-hour trip to catch an hour or so of sleep. Both times she found a lighted parking lot in a mall and slept in the locked cab of the truck with her Winchester by her side.

She passed through Midland, stopping at the post office to check her mail and was almost past the entrance to the Marriott when she noticed her Suburban and the other two *Circle R* trucks in the parking lot. Carrie stopped and had to back up to the entrance to pull into the hotel driveway. Thanks to the desk clerk, she found a few of the guys in the bar. When she asked what was going on, they told her the same story they had given Lowery. That was yesterday, they said, and they were getting tired of hanging out in the hotel. They wanted to know when they could go home, and did she know what was going on out there? She told them to stay put and headed for the ranch.

Carrie left the hotel heading for the front entrance but, at the last minute, thought better of it. Cal and Skip wouldn't have come back and evacuated her ranch unless they were sure of some kind of trouble, and she was not about to walk into the middle of it. She drove the half-mile to the back entrance and parked halfway in, quickly unloading and saddling Spider. Carrie kicked him into a gallop.

She came around the corner of the main house just as Sullivan shot Lowery. Instinctively, she pulled the Winchester out of its scabbard. She had used it to kill animals for food and to protect the livestock. The idea of looking down the sights of a rifle at a human had never entered her mind but, when the man started to raise the pistol to point it at Cal, she stood in the stirrups and fired without thinking. She lowered the rifle and slowly sank back in the saddle as the man fell to his knees and then to the ground. She couldn't take her eyes off the dark puddle growing in the sand around his body. She stayed in that position until Cal called to her as he helped his daughter onto the porch.

She turned, and they looked at each other for a long moment. Finally, she said, "Bring her inside."

She slid from Spider's back to the porch and realized that both Cal and Traci were staring at the gun in her hand. She looked at it as if it were a foreign object and quickly put it down on the porch swing.

After the ambulance left, the Midland police and Detective Martini took statements from everyone before returning to town. Cal, Skip, and Traci stayed at the ranch that night. Cal and Carrie talked late into the night as he told her who he was and all that had happened. The last time he saw her, she was standing on her porch as they drove away.

Back in New York, Cal thought of her standing there, watching them go. He had tried for a year, but he now knew he could not live here in his old life without Jan. He had been back at work for almost eight months, but his heart was not in it. His decision to leave was in the making since he returned from the wedding. He sat down with Skip and told him he was leaving both the company and the city. It was an emotional meeting for both men but, in the end, Skip understood.

Cal turned off the lights and walked away from the life he had known for the last thirty years. As far as he was concerned, it died with Jan in a courtyard in Las Cruces, New Mexico.

* * * * *

It was unseasonably hot for October, Carrie thought. She finished putting fresh hay in the feed basket of each stall. Now she was wet with sweat, and hay stuck to her everywhere. The crew had been at work since early in the morning and were starting to slow down for the day. She wasn't sure which she was looking forward to the most, taking a long shower or sitting in the swing with an ice-cold Heineken in her hand. She hung up the pitchfork and left the barn for the main house. Halfway across the compound, she noticed the taxicab. Cal was standing on the porch watching her. He had called her twice after the shootings to thank her and to see how she was doing. She followed the trials and heard about Traci's wedding on the news but, for the most part, she tried not to think about him. She had not been successful. He would creep into her thoughts in the middle of the day, and he would slip into her dreams at night. She often wondered what he was doing and how he was coping with his loss. She stopped a few feet from the porch.

"This is a surprise," was all she could manage.

"Well, I left New York for good. I think I'm going to try to find work out here. You know, I kind of got hooked on the ranch life when I was staying here." Cal shifted from one foot to the other and hesitated for a minute. "I thought I would stop and see you since I was passing by."

She looked down for a moment and then spoke. "I think you know how I feel. I've always wanted you here," she said, as she searched his face.

"I won't lie to you about my feelings; I've been in love with Jan my whole life. I will love her until I die, but you and I both know something happened between us when I was here." Cal held her eyes as he spoke. "I went back home and tried to live my old life; that's not going to happen. My feelings for you have not changed, Carrie. I thought about you and the ranch a lot."

Carrie looked at the ground and scuffed it with her foot for a long time before she spoke again.

"If you want work, there is always plenty to do here. You can start tomorrow." she offered.

Cal watched her for a long moment, and she held his gaze. He smiled. "That sounds good, boss."

"Okay. But right now I need a shower, and it would be great if you had a couple of cold ones waiting when I come down. You remember where the kitchen is, I trust?" she said, grinning.

"I think I can find it," he said. "Maybe later we can saddle the horses and head up to the ridge," Cal said, as he followed her inside.

Tom Blenk

168

About the Author

Tom Blenk, 50, has been a postal worker in Exeter, New Hampshire for more than thirty years, having lived in and around the area for forty-five years. He comes from a large family of eight kids and has been married for over thirty years to his wife, Barbara. He is an avid fan of all sports, including being an avid golfer and, more importantly, a high school football coach for eleven years, the past six at Exeter High School. He enjoys traveling, a wide spectrum of music, movies and reading (wide variety of topics, including Military History).

This is Mr. Blenk's first novel. He got the idea for the story and started writing in September of 1999. After reading Stephen King's book *On Writing* and rewriting his own book twice he finally had a finished product in late November 2001.

Printed in the United States
712800004B